喚醒你的英文語感！

Get a Feel for English !

喚醒你的英文語感！

Get a Feel for English !

BIZ ENGLISH FOR BUSY PEOPLE

Job

愈忙愈要學

求職英文

風行 500 大企業的 Leximodel 字串學習法

BIZ ENGLISH
for
BUSY PEOPLE

在國際能力和自我推銷掛帥的時代，
無論個人的能力、資歷或求職技巧，
無一不是微利時代企業的選才取向，
只要熟悉本書的寫作、口說雙管齊下、
履歷、求職信、面試三效合一的字串，
就業市場通行無阻，職場達人非你莫屬！

附1片實戰 MP3

貝塔語言出版
Beta Multimedia Publishing

作者◎商英教父 Quentin Brand

Contents 目錄

Unit 1　履歷表

Unit 2　求職信

Part 2 求職面試篇

Unit 3　準備面試

Contents

Preface ⓪

前言
The Leximodel

引言與學習目標

在國際公司謀得一職從來沒有比現在更簡單，也從來沒有比現在更艱難了。在全球化的快速發展之下，不僅位於台灣或中國的外商分公司提供的工作機會與日俱增，全球化也影響了招聘和企業獵才等服務產業。企業獵才服務公司和其他招聘公司越來越常從當地人才庫以外的地方尋覓適當的主管人選，因此受聘到國外從事有趣工作的機會可不低。不過反而觀之，有意進入外商公司發展國際事業的商界人士有增無減，求職者之間的競爭想必也益發白熱化。在商界中，英文向來是眾家網羅人才和向雇主展現才幹的標準語言，而在招聘公司的眼中，求職者技能和經歷的呈現能力更是選擇人才的關鍵所在。

各位的商業能力和經驗或許優異有加，甚至用英語寫電子郵件、開會、寫報告和做簡報等商業任務亦非難事，然而在求職過程中英文若沒有達到水準之上，人資部和招聘公司的人還是不大可能多看你一眼的。

大家在用英文求職的過程中屢戰屢敗的原因有三。首先，相較於商業英語的其他用途，用英文撰寫簡歷表或履歷表、求職信或參加面試，可說是截然不同。第二，這類英文的語法特殊且使用機會不多，因此練習不易，不像每天上班幾乎都得寫電子郵件和做簡報，遲早會上手，你可不會一天到晚都在找工作吧（但願如此）！第三，這類英文所冒的成敗風險較高。若有一份你急欲得到的工作，面試時就已步步為營，還得額外承受用外語面試的精神壓力，無論在字詞的發音、聽力和記憶力等各方面都會受到影響。

本書要做的便是幫助各位通過層層關卡、過關斬將。教會各位求職過程中的重要英文須知，並且示範如何將這些知識應用在你個人的情況和才幹上，最後再讓各位練習運用這類英文，在求職時更得心應手，找到理想工作的機會也跟著提高！

為了讓各位更輕易有效地將本書的內容應用在個人的經驗和需求上，本書將以兩名求職中的虛構人物為例。

凱文的事業才剛起步。他年約二十出頭，大學主修商科，馬上就要完成大學學業。他在上大學之前已經當過兵，所以正摩拳擦掌準備踏入職場。他的畢業論文是以大中華地區（Greater China）的行銷策略為題，主要探討跨文化行銷法（cross-cultural marketing）如何向華人消費者推銷西方品牌。他在學校放假期間，曾經在不同的零售店當過售貨員，對業務已有一些經驗，此外還在學校當過社團的出納股長，對財務方面也小有經驗。至於凱文深入的背景和經驗，將在 Unit 1 再向各位介紹。

黛西正值事業的發展中期。她三十幾歲，單身沒有小孩，有三個兄弟姐妹能照顧父母。她在金融界有十年的會計經驗，曾經待過的公司有國內的也有國際的。她的經歷包括幫國內公司辦理退稅和財務決算，也協助過外商公司處理有關台灣稅法方面的事宜。此外，她還曾透過不同的國際稅制幫助客戶降低稅務成本。她曾經為加入會計師協會而到英國留學一年，現在正在攻讀商業管理碩士學位。在 Unit 1 中也會告訴各位更多關於黛西的背景和經歷。

建議各位可以專攻本書中最符合自己年齡和經歷的內容，不過別忘了本書的其他內容對各位可能也會有所幫助，尤其是 Part 1 和 Part 2 的引言部分。

現在請先花一點時間閱讀下面方框中的問題，並寫下答案。於作答時，請先暫時別往下閱讀，待作答完畢後再繼續閱讀。

Task　1

請思考以下問題，寫下自己的答案。

> 1. 你購買本書的原因為何？你希望從本書學到什麼？
> 2. 在未來用英文求職的過程中，你覺得可能會遇到哪些困難？
> 3. 在過去用英文求職的過程中，你曾經遇到哪些困難？

從以下針對上述問題所提出的答案選項，勾選出最貼近自己想法和情況的答案。

1. 你購買本書的原因為何？你希望從本書學到什麼？
   - ❏ 購買這本書是由於我即將大學畢業，而且希望能在外商公司謀得一份好差事。所以需要學習履歷表和求職信的撰寫秘訣，將我的大學經歷，以吸引人力資源部注意的方式呈現出來。此外，我也需要學會用英文參加面試的技巧。

☐ 購買這本書是由於我想在事業上更上一層樓。我在國內幾家公司工作多年，獲得許多紮實且難得的經驗，現在該是往國際公司發展和拓展視野的時候了。因此，我需要一些撰寫英文履歷和求職信的提點，以及應試方面的協助。

☐ 購買這本書是因為我相中了一份在外商公司的職位，我赴任的意願非常高。無論是在國內公司或外商公司，我都有多年的商務經驗。我所需要的協助是，能夠寫出出眾的履歷和求職信，而且在英文面試時不致令我的表現扣分。畢竟，這份職缺是我千載難逢的機會。

☐ 購買過此系列的其他本書，覺得這套英文教學法不僅實際而且有效。因此，希望藉由這本書加強我既有的商用英文能力。此外，也想學會面試時必備的自我介紹方式，期望自己能表現出自信但不驕傲的態度，同時，學會履歷表的國際通用寫法和一般風格，對個人未來的謀職或轉職應該大有助益。

2. 在未來用英文求職的過程中，你覺得可能會遇到哪些困難？

☐ 由於才剛進入職場，所以不太清楚怎麼做才能符合對方的期望。我也不清楚履歷和求職信的正確撰寫格式。這是我第一次求職，我不希望我的履歷表或求職信看起來不夠專業或不夠誠懇。我想我未來可能會遇到的問題之一，就是想展現專業形象卻不知從何著手。

☐ 由於我正處於職場生涯的起跑點上，想說服雇主我具備應付現實商業環境的能力並不容易。所以，我需要讓對方知道，我在大學的經驗不僅派得上用場，並且和商界的工作也有相關，況且我個人的特質也足以彌補經驗上的不足。我相信我會學得很快，只差對方給我一個機會展現！

☐ 我不太清楚面試會遇到哪些狀況，也不知道對方會問哪些問題，而我又該如何應對。總之，我沒有把握要符合對方的哪些要求才算是面試成功。

☐ 我知道我在面試時會非常緊張，必須在面試前勤加演練才行。不管是聽力或口說能力，我對自己的英文沒有十足的把握，無法確定能否應付用英文面試。

3. 在過去用英文求職的過程中，你曾經遇到哪些困難？

☐ 我不知道如何將履歷表寫得讓人眼睛為之一亮。我所從事的行業競爭相當激烈，同一份工作有許多競爭對手。所以我的履歷表必須展現出令人難忘的印象及說服力。過去我在這方面不甚成功，全因我的英文能力不夠好，寫不出亮眼的履歷。

❑ 我過去曾經遇到的問題之一，就是不知該如何依特定職務量身訂做合適的履歷表。我的商務經驗廣泛，而且我希望讓人力資源部知道我的某些經驗可以應用在應徵的工作領域上，但卻不知如何用英文達到此一目的。

❑ 撰寫求職信對我而言是最困難的部分，因為寫作並非我的強項。我不知道如何針對各個不同的公司和職務需求來撰寫求職信。

❑ 我在面試時往往會非常害羞，因為我不大懂得自我介紹和推銷。中國文化講求謙遜，但在面試時卻得展現出自己的技能和才幹，自信與謙虛之間不易拿捏。

❑ 對我來說，面試時能用對字、說對話是最艱難的部分。要是找不到適當的字詞來形容的話，回答的就不夠完整。我知道談吐有自信，面試時才會留給對方好印象。我個性不算害羞，只是不知道如何用英文表達意思，要是用中文表達的話就不成問題了！

各位可能部分或完全同意以上這幾點理由，也可能另有其他上面沒有提到的答案。不過先容我先在此做個自我介紹。

我是 Quentin Brand，已經教了超過十五年的英文，對象包括來自世界各地像各位這樣的商界專業人士，而且我有好幾年的時間都待在台灣。客戶包括企業各階層人士，從大型跨國企業國外分公司的經理，到擁有海外市場的小型本地公司所雇用的基層實習生不等。我所教過的學生中有初學者，也有英文程度非常高的人，以及許多程度介於兩者之間各行各業的人士，我發現學習求職這方面知識的人，不僅包括求職者本身，還有需要用英文面試他人的人力資源部員工。

多年來，我開發了一套教導和學習英文的方法，專門幫各位這樣忙碌的商界人士解決疑慮。這套辦法的核心概念稱作 Leximodel，是一種以嶄新角度看待英語的教學法。目前 Leximodel 已經獲得全世界一些大型頂尖企業所採用，以協助企業主管充分發揮本身具備的英語潛能，而本書就是以 Leximodel 為基礎。

本章的目的在於介紹 Leximodel 的概念，以及其運用方式。同時，也針對如何藉由本書將這套學習法發揮至最大效用來加以說明。

閱讀完本章之後，各位應該能夠達成的學習目標如下：

❑ 清楚了解 Leximodel 的概念，以及它對各位在學習上有什麼好處。
❑ 了解 chunks 、 set-phrases 和 word partnerships 的差別。
❑ 在任何文章中能自行找出 chunks 、 set-phrases 和 word partnerships 。
❑ 清楚了解學習 set-phrases 的困難點，以及如何克服這些困難。
❑ 清楚了解本書中的不同要素，以及如何將這些要素加以運用。

但在繼續下面的章節之前，先談談 Task 在本書的重要性。各位在 Task 1 可以看到，我請各位先針對一些問題寫下自己的答案。希望各位都能按照我所說的步驟，先做完 Task 再往下閱讀。

每一單元都有許多經過嚴謹設計的 Task ，可以協助各位在潛移默化中吸收新的語言。此外，在做 Task 時的思維過程要比答對與否來得重要，因此各位在練習時請務必按照既定的順序進行，且在做完練習之前先不要參看答案。

當然，為了節省時間，各位也可以略過 Task 、一鼓作氣把整本書看完。不過，這麼做反而會造成時間上的浪費，因為沒有做好必要的思維工作，本書就無法發揮其最大效果。請相信我的話，按部就班地做 Task 準沒錯。

The Leximodel

可預測度

在本節中，要向各位介紹的是 Leximodel 學習法。 Leximodel 是一種看待語言的新方法，而且是以一個很簡單的概念爲基礎，那就是：

> **Language consists of words which appear with other words.**
> 語言是由字串所構成。

這種說法簡單易懂。 Leximodel 的基礎概念是從字串的層面來看語言，而非以文法和單字的層面來看語言。爲了讓各位明白這個概念，讓我們先來做 Task 2 吧！做完練習之前請先不要往下閱讀。

Task 2

想一想，下列單字後面通常都會搭配什麼字？請寫在空格中。

listen _____

depend _____

English _____

financial _____

各位很可能會在第一個字後面填上 to ，在第二個字後面填上 on 。我猜得沒錯吧？因爲只要用一套叫做 corpus linguistics 的軟體程式和運算技術，就可以發現在統計上 listen 後面接 to 的機率非常高（大約是 98.9%），而 depend 後面接 on 的機率也差不多如此。這表示 listen 和 depend 後面所接的字幾乎是千篇一律，不會改變（listen 接 to ； depend 接 on）。由於伴隨出現的機率非常高，所以我們可以把這兩

個片語（listen to、depend on）視為固定（fixed）字串。正由於它們伴隨出現的情況是固定的，所以假若各位所寫的不是 to 和 on，就可說是寫錯了。

不過，接下來的兩個字（English、financial）後面會接什麼字就難預測得多，所以我猜不出各位在這兩個字的後面寫了什麼。但我可以在某個特定範圍內進行猜測，在 English 後面可能寫的是 class、book、teacher、email 或 grammar 等字；而在 financial 後面寫的是 department、news、planning、product、problems 或 stability 等字。但我猜對的把握就比前面兩個字低了許多。為什麼會這樣？因為 English 和 financial 後面接的字有很多可能組合，而且伴隨出現的機率也都相當，所以猜對的準確率低了許多。因此，我們可以說 English 和 financial 的字串不是固定的，而是流動的（fluid）。所以，與其把語言想成是由文法和單字構成的，不妨把語言想成是一個龐大的字串語料庫；裡面有些字串是固定的，有些字串則是流動的。

總而言之，根據可預測度我們可以看出字串的固定性和流動性，如下圖所示：

The Spectrum of Predictability 可預測度

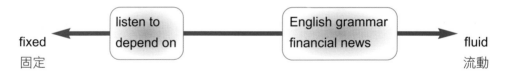

字串的可預測度是 Leximodel 的基礎，因此 Leximodel 的定義可以追加一句：

Language consists of words which appear with other words. These combinations of words can be placed along a spectrum of predictability, with fixed combinations at one end, and fluid combinations at the other.

語言由字串所構成。每個字串根據可預測度來加以區分，可預測度愈高的一端是固定字串，可預測度愈低的一端是流動字串。

Chunks、set-phrases 和 word partnerships

　　各位可能在心裡兀自納悶：我曉得 Leximodel 是什麼了，可是這對學英文有何幫助？我如何知道哪些是固定字串，哪些又是流動字串？況且，就算能夠分辨，對學英文來說會比較簡單嗎？別急，放輕鬆，從今天開始，英文就會愈學愈上手！

　　我們可以把所有的字串（稱之為 MWIs = multi-word items）分為三類：chunks、set-phrases 和 word partnerships。這些字沒有對等的中文譯名，所以請各位要記住這幾個英文字。現在，讓我們仔細來看這三類字串，各位很快就會發現它們真的很容易理解，使用上也很方便。

　　我們先來看第一類 MWIs：chunks。Chunks 字串有固定的也有流動的，listen to 就是個好例子：listen 的後面總是跟著 to（這是固定的），但有時候 listen 可以是 are listening、listened 或 have not been listening carefully enough（這些是流動的）。另一個好例子則是 give sth. to sb.。其中的 give 總是先接某物（sth.），然後再接 to，最後再接某人（sb.）。就這點來說，它是固定的。不過在這個 chunk 中，sth. 和 sb. 這兩個部分可以選擇的字很多，像是 give a raise to your staff（給員工加薪）和 give a presentation to your boss（向老闆做簡報）。從下列圖示各位應該不難理解：

相信各位也能夠舉一反三想出更多的例子。當然，我們還可以把 give sth. to sb. 寫成 give sb. sth.，但這就變成了另一個 chunk。由此各位可看出 chunk 兼具固定和流動的元素。

而且 chunks 通常很短，是由 meaning words（意義字，如 listen、depend）加上 function words（功能字，如 to、on）所組成。相信各位認得的 chunks 並不算少，只是渾然不知罷了！所以，我們可以再來做另一個 Task，看看各位是不是已經懂得 chunks 的組成元素。請務必先作完 Task 3 再看答案，千萬不能作弊喔！

Task 3

請閱讀下列短文，找出所有的 chunks 並畫上底線。

Everyone is familiar with the experience of knowing what a word means, but not knowing how to use it accurately in a sentence. This is because words are nearly always used as part of an MWI. There are three kinds of MWI. The first is called a chunk. A chunk is a combination of words that is more or less fixed. Every time a word in the chunk is used, it must be used with its partner(s). Chunks combine fixed and fluid elements of language. When you learn a new word, you should learn the chunk. There are thousands of chunks in English. One way you can help yourself to improve your English is by noticing and keeping a database of the chunks you find as you read. You should also try to memorize as many as possible.

每個人都有這樣的經驗：知道一個字的意思，卻不知道如何正確用在句子當中，這是因為每個字幾乎都必須當作是 MWI 的一部分。而 MWI 可分為三類，第一類叫做 chunk。Chunk 的組成幾乎算是固定不變的，每當用到 chunk 的其中一字，該字的詞夥也得一併用上。此外，Chunks 也包含了語言中的固定元素和流動元素。在學習新字時，應該連帶學會它的 chunk。英文中有成千上萬的 chunks。各位在閱讀時多加留意並記下所有的 chunks，將之彙整成語庫，最好還要盡量背起來，才不失為加強英文的好法子。

Task　3　▶參考答案

　　現在將所寫的答案與下面所列的語庫加以比較。假如沒有找到那麼多的 chunks，那就再讀一次短文，看看是否能在文中找到語庫裡所有的 chunks。

求職必備語庫 前言 1

- ... be familiar with n.p. ...
- ... experience of Ving ...
- ... how to V ...
- ... be used as n.p. ...
- ... part of n.p. ...
- ... there are ...
- ... kinds of n.p. ...
- ... the first ...
- ... be called n.p. ...
- ... a combination of n.p. ...
- ... more or less ...
- ... every time + clause ...
- ... be used with n.p. ...
- ... combine sth. and sth. ...
- ... elements of n.p. ...
- ... thousands of n.p. ...
- ... in English ...
- ... help yourself to V ...
- ... keep a database of n.p. ...
- ... try to V ...
- ... as many as ...
- ... as many as possible ...

■ 語庫小叮嚀

- 語庫中的 chunks，be 動詞都以原形 be 表示，而非 is 或 are。
- 記下 chunks 時，前後都要加上 ...（刪節號）。
- 有些 chunks 後面接 V（如：go、write 等原形動詞）或 Ving（如：going、writing 等），有的則接 n.p.（noun phrase，名詞片語）或 clause（子句）。這些將在「本書使用說明」中詳加解說。

　　好的，接下來我們要看的是第二類 MWIs：set-phrases。Set-phrases 比 chunks 固定，通常字串較長，其中可能含有好幾個 chunks。而 set-phrases 通常有個開頭或結尾，或是兩者皆有，這表示完整的句子有時候也可以是 set-phrase。但 chunks 通常是由沒頭沒尾的片斷文字所組成。至於 set-phrases 則常見於寫 email 時的用語。現在請參考下列語庫並做 Task 4。

Task 4

請看下列寫 email 時常見的 set-phrases，將你認得的勾選出來。

求職必備語庫 前言 2

- ❏ Thank you for sending me n.p. ...
- ❏ Apologies for the delay in getting back to you, but ...
- ❏ Thanks for your reply.
- ❏ Just to let you know that + clause ...
- ❏ Just to confirm that + clause ...
- ❏ Please confirm that + clause ...
- ❏ I look forward to hearing from you.
- ❏ If you have any queries, please do not hesitate to call either ... or ...
- ❏ If you have any questions about this, please do not hesitate to contact me.

══ 語庫小叮嚀

- ■ 由於 set-phrases 是三類字串中固定性最高的，因此在學習時務必特別留意 set-phrases 的每個細節。稍後將針對此點詳加說明。
- ■ 有些 set-phrases 以 n.p. 結尾，有的則以 clause 結尾。稍後也將詳加解說此點。

學會 set-phrases 的好處在於，使用時不必考慮文法：只需將這些 set-phrases 以固定字串的形式背起來，原原本本地照用即可。本書大部分的 Task 都和 set-phrases 有關，將於下一節對此詳加解說。現在，讓我們再繼續看第三類的 MWIs: word partnerships。

這三類 MWIs 中，以 word partnerships 的流動性最高，word partnerships 含有二個以上的意義字（不同於 chunks 的只含意義字和功能字），而且通常是「動詞＋形容詞＋名詞」或「名詞＋名詞」的組合。 Word partnerships 會隨行業或談論的話題而有所改變，但各個產業所用的 chunks 和 set-phrases 都一樣。舉例來說，如果在製藥業工作，用到的 word partnerships 就會跟在資訊科技業服務的人士有所不同。現在，請各位接著做下面的 Task 5，就會瞭解我所說的意思。

Task 5

請依據範例，將會使用到下列各組 word partnerships 的產業寫出來。

❶
- government regulations
- patient response
- key opinion leader
- drug trial
- hospital budget
- patent law

產業名稱：＿＿＿製藥業＿＿＿

❷
- risk assessment
- credit rating
- low inflation
- non-performing loan
- share price index
- bond portfolio

產業名稱：＿＿＿＿＿＿＿＿＿

❸
- bill of lading
- customs delay
- letter of credit
- shipment details
- shipping date
- customer service

產業名稱：＿＿＿＿＿＿＿＿＿

❹
- latest technology
- system problem
- input data
- user interface
- repetitive strain injury
- installation wizard

產業名稱：＿＿＿＿＿＿＿＿＿

Task 5 ▶參考答案

❷ 銀行和金融業
❸ 外銷／進出口業
❹ 資訊科技業

假如各位在上述產業服務，一定認得出其中一些 word partnerships。

所以，現在我們對 Leximodel 的定義應該要再修正如下：

Language consists of words which appear with other words. These combinations can be categorized as chunks, set-phrases, and word partnerships, and placed along a spectrum of predictability, with fixed combinations at one end, and fluid combinations at the other.

語言由字串構成，所有的字串可以分成三大類——chunks、set-phrases 和 word partnerships，並且可依其可預測的程度區分，可預測度愈高的一端是固定字串，可預測度愈低的一端是流動字串。

所以，新的 Leximodel 可以圖示如下：

The Spectrum of Predictability 可預測度

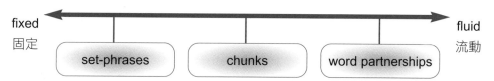

此外，只要致力學好 chunks，文法就會有所精進，因為大部分的文法錯誤其實都源自於 chunks 寫錯；若專攻 set-phrases，英語的使用功能就會增強，因為 set-phrases 都是功能性字串；若在 word partnerships 下功夫，字彙量就會擴增。因此，最後的 Leximodel 就可圖示如下：

The Spectrum of Predictability 可預測度

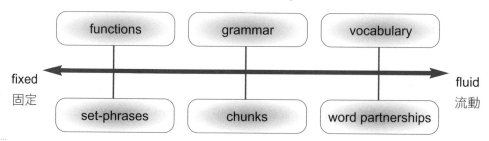

Leximodel 的優點及其對於學習英文的妙用，就在於說、寫英文時，均無須再為文法規則傷透腦筋。學習英文時，首要之務是建立 chunks、set-phrases 和 word partnerships 的語料庫，多學多益。而不是死背文法規則，還得苦思如何將單字套用到文法中。這三類 MWIs 用來輕而易舉，而且更符合人腦記憶和使用語言的習慣。現在，我們再來做最後一個 Task，以確認完全了解 Leximodel 的概念，並驗證這項學習法的簡單好用。切記在完成 Task 之前，先不要看語庫。

Task　6

　　請看以下這封求職信和其譯文，然後以三種不同顏色的筆分別將所有的 chunks、set-phrases 和 word partnerships 畫上底線。最後，請依各類字串的範例完成下頁的分類表。各位還可以利用本書所附的 MP3 音檔，聽取這封求職信的有聲版來練習口說，或依此錄製屬於你自己的有聲版求職信。

Dear Sir/Madam,

I am writing in connection with the advertisement in the *Taipei Times* 14 March 2002.

You will see from my attached CV that I am an experienced accountant, with more than eight years practical experience — much of this time with international companies located in Taipei. Although at the moment I am working as an auditor[1] for A Very Big Local Accounting Company Ltd. (AVBLAC Ltd.), I would like to expand my international experience. I am currently in the final stages of my MBA in international tax law and intend to make offshore[2] taxation the subject of my dissertation.[3]

I believe I am suitably qualified and experienced for the job advertised. I would be interested in talking with you further about the job.

I look forward to hearing from you.

Word List

1 auditor [ˋɔdɪtə] *n.* 查帳員，稽核員　　3 dissertation [ˌdɪsəˋteʃən] *n.* 論文
2 offshore[ˋɔfˋʃor] *a.* 境外的

敬啓者：

在 2002 年 3 月 14 日的《台北時報》看到貴公司的徵人啓事，謹來函應徵。

由附上的履歷表您可看到我具備豐富的會計經驗，除了有長達八年以上的實務歷練之外，還有一段很長的時間是為多家位於台北的國際公司效力。現於 A Very Big Local Accounting Company Ltd.（簡稱 AVBLAC Ltd.）擔任稽核員一職，仍望擴展自己的國際經驗，是以所攻讀的國際稅法商管碩士學位現已達最後階段，畢業論文則計畫以國際稅法為題。

本人自信符合貴公司刊登之職務的資歷要求，望能進一步討論此職務之相關事宜。

靜候佳音。

set-phrases	chunks	word partnerships
I am writing in connection with ...	*... the advertisement in ...*	*experienced accountant*

Task 6 ▶參考答案

請利用下面的必備語庫來核對答案。

求職必備語庫 前言 3

set-phrases	chunks	word partnerships
I am writing in connection with ...	... the advertisement in ...	experienced accountant
You will see from my attached CV that ...	... much of this time ...	practical experience
I would like to expand n.p. ...	... located in ...	international companies
I believe I am ...	... at the moment ...	international experience
I would be interested in ...	... working as ...	international tax law
I look forward to hearing from you.	... in the final stages of ...	offshore taxation
	... intend to ...	final dissertation
	... talking with sb. about sth. ...	

■ 語庫小叮嚀

- ■ Set-phrases 通常以大寫開頭,或以句號結尾。而刪節號(...)則代表句子的流動部分。
- ■ Chunks 的開頭和結尾都有刪節號,表示 chunks 為句子的中間部分。
- ■ Word partnerships 均由兩個以上的意義字所組成。

　　假如各位寫出的答案沒有這麼完整,不必擔心。只要多加練習,就能找出文中所有的固定元素。不過有一件事是可以確定的:等到各位能找出這麼多 MWIs 時,就表示英文程度已經到達登峰造極的境界了!相信各位很快便能擁有這樣的英文能力。讀完本書後,我會請各位再做一次這個 Task,來驗證自己的學習成果。如果有時間的話,各位不妨找一篇英文文章,像是英文母語人士所寫的電子郵件,或是雜誌和網路上的文章,然後用它來做同樣的練習,想必定能熟能生巧哦!

 # 本書使用說明

截至目前為止，我想各位大概會覺得 Leximodel 似乎是個不錯的概念，但仍有滿腹疑問，對吧？對於各位可能會有的問題，我來看看能否提供解答。

● 我該如何實際運用 Leximodel 學英文？為什麼 Leximodel 和我以前碰到的英文教學法截然不同？

簡而言之，我的答案是：只要知道字詞的組合和這些組合的固定程度，就能簡化英語學習的過程，同時大幅減少犯錯的機率。

以前的教學法要各位學好文法，然後套用句子，邊寫邊造句。用這方法寫作不僅有如牛步，而且稍不小心便錯誤百出，想必各位早就有切身體驗了。現在只要用 Leximodel 建立 chunks、set-phrases 和 word partnerships 語庫，接著只需背起來就能學會英文寫作了。

● 這本書如何以 Leximodel 教學？

本書除了提供履歷表、求職信和工作面試中最常見的固定字串（chunks、set-phrases 和 word partnerships，但絕大多數是 set-phrases）之外，並教各位如何留意和記下每天所看到的英文，來增強英文基礎。本書所附的 MP3 也可提供各位隨聽隨學的輔助。

● 為什麼要留意字串中所有的字，這一點很重要嗎？

不知何故，大多數人對眼前的英文視而不見，分明擺在面前卻仍然視若無睹，時常緊盯著字詞的意思，卻忽略了傳達字義的方法。雖然每天所瀏覽的固定 MWI 多不勝數，但其實這些 MWI 只不過是組成固定而又反覆出現的字串罷了。很多其他種類的語言都有這種現象。不如我們就來做個實驗吧，各位就會知道我說的是真是假。現在請做下面的 Task 7。

Task　7

請看下列的 set-phrases，並選出正確的。

❑ Regarding the report you sent me ...
❑ Regarding to the report you sent me ...
❑ Regards to the report you sent me ...
❑ With regards the report you sent ...
❑ To regard the report you sent me ...
❑ Regard to the report you sent me ...

姑且不論所選的答案爲何，我敢說各位一定覺得這題很難作答。我們可能每天都會看到或聽到這個 set-phrase，卻從來沒有仔細留意它當中的每一個字（其實第一個 set-phrase 是正確答案，其餘都是錯的！）。說到這兒，以下是我要給各位學習 set-phrase 時的第一個忠告：

雖然各位應該對所接觸的英文加強注意，但仿效的文字則必須出自以英文爲母語的人士之手。所謂的「以英文爲母語的人士」，指的是美國人、英國人、澳洲人、紐西蘭人、加拿大人或南非人。除了這些來源的英語可供仿效之外，其他來源的英語可信度都不夠。因此，爲了擴增各位的字串語庫，本書所提供的學習英語基本原則就是：「務必只仿效英文母語人士的用語示範」。

如果多留意每天接觸到的固定字串，久而久之一定會記起來，轉化成自己英文基礎的一部分，這可是諸多文獻可考的事實。只需多加留意閱讀時所遇到的 MWI，亦可提升學習效率。Leximodel 正是以幫助各位達到這一點爲目標。

● 需要小心哪些問題？

本書中設計許多 Task 的目的，即在於幫助各位克服學習 set-phrases 時所遇到的問題。至於學習 set-phrases 的要領就在於：「務必留意 set-phrases 中的所有字」。

從 Task 7 中，各位或許已發現自己其實不如想像中那麼仔細留意 set-phrases 中的所有字。接下來要更明確地告訴各位學習 set-phrases 時的注意事項，這些注意事項對於學習 set-phrases 而言非常重要，所以切勿草率閱讀。學習和使用 set-phrases 時，需要注意的細節有四大類：

❶ 短字（如 a、the、to、in、at、on 和 but）。這些字很難記，但瞭解這點之後，便可說是跨出了一大步。由於 set-phrases 極爲固定，用錯一個短字，整個 set-phrase 都會改變，等於是寫錯了。

❷ 字尾（有些字的字尾是 -ed，有些是 -ing，有些則是 -ment，此外有些字尾要加 -s，有些字尾則不加 -s）。字尾改變，字的意思也會隨之改變。由於 set-phrase 極爲固定，寫錯其中一字的字尾，整個 set-phrase 都會改變，也等於是寫錯了。

❸ 完整的 set-phrases。Set-phrase 是固定的單位，所以必須完整地加以使用，不能只用前半部或其中幾個字而已。

❹ Set-phrases 的結尾（有的 set-phrases 以 clause 結尾，有的以 n.p. 結尾，有的以 V 結尾，有的則以 Ving 結尾），我們稱之爲 code。許多人犯錯，問題即出在句子中的 set-phrases 與其他部分的銜接。學習 set-phrases 時，必須將 code 當作 set-phrases 的一部分一併背起來。由於 set-phrases 極爲固定，code 寫錯，整個 set-phrase 都會改變，亦等於是寫錯了。

說明至此，請再做下面的 Task 8，以確認各位能夠掌握 code 的用法。

Task 8

請看以下對 code 的定義，然後將列出的字串分門別類填入表格中。其中已將第一個字串所屬的類別示範如下。

■ clause = （子句），各位在學校大概已經學過，clause 一定包含主詞和動詞。例如：I need your help.、She is on leave.、We are closing the department.、What is your estimate? 等。

- n. p.　= noun phrase（名詞片語），這其實就是 word partnership，不含動詞或主詞。例如： financial news 、 cost reduction 、 media review data 、 joint stock company 等。

- V　　= verb（動詞）。和 clause 的不同之處在於， V 不包含主詞。

- Ving　= verb ending in -ing（以 -ing 結尾的動詞）。以前各位的老師可能稱之爲動名詞，但 Ving 只是看起來像名詞的動詞。

• ~~bill of lading~~	• having	• our market share
• customer complaint	• he is not	• see
• decide	• help	• sending
• did you remember	• helping	• talking
• do	• I'm having a meeting	• we need some more data
• doing	• John wants to see you	• wrong figures
• go	• knowing	• you may remember
• great presentation	• look after	• your new client

clause	n.p.	V	Ving
	• *bill of lading*		

Task 8 ▶參考答案

請利用下面的必備語庫來核對答案。

求 職 必 備 語 庫 前言 4

clause	n.p.	V	Ving
• did you remember	• bill of lading	• decide	• doing
• he is not	• customer complaint	• do	• having
• I'm having a meeting	• great presentation	• go	• helping
• John wants to see you	• our market share	• help	• knowing
• we need some more data	• wrong figures	• look after	• sending
• you may remember	• your new client	• see	• talking

▰ 語庫小叮嚀

■ clause（子句）的 verb（動詞）前面一定要有主詞。

■ noun phrases（名詞片語）基本上即為 word partnerships。

總而言之，學習 set-phrases 時，容易出錯的主要問題有：

1. 短字
2. 字尾
3. 完整的 set-phrase
4. Set-phrases 的結尾

並不會太困難，對吧？剛剛介紹給各位的 set-phrases 相關知識，大部分的 chunks 也都適用。不過在使用 chunks 時，請注意其中的流動元素是否正確。例如：使用動詞 chunk 時，必須檢查動詞的時態；使用名詞 chunk 時，則必須注意 chunk 是否為加上 -s 的複數型，以及檢查其冠詞或限定詞是否無誤。

● 若沒有文法規則可循，我如何得知自己的 set-phrases 和 chunks 用法正確無誤？

　　關於這點，其實並不困難。本書所包含的必備語庫，就是專為幫助各位達到此點而設計的。各位只須檢查履歷表或求職信，確定其中用到的 set-phrases 或 chunks 和必備語庫中的完全一致即可。至於口說方面，請於練習 set-phrases 或 chunks 時，特別留意其發音。只要專心聆聽連音部分和音調等細微之處，以確定自己的 set-phrases 聽起來和本書所附之 MP3 光碟中的完全一致即可。

　　因此，學習 set-phrases 的時候，只要專心學習書中的必備語庫和 MP3 中的音檔就好，不必擔心文法規則。雖然說來簡單，事實上也確實如此，畢竟熟能生巧準沒錯。現在請再做下面的 Task 9，記住，做完之後才往下看答案。

Task　9

　　請看以下的句子，並和「必備語庫前言 3」中的 set-phrases 作比較。各位能看出兩者有什麼不同嗎？在以下每個句子的下面寫出正確的句子，並在右欄標示出該句的錯誤原因編號（錯誤的原因有：1. 短字；2. 字尾；3. 完整的 set-phrase；4. set-phrases 的結尾）。請見第一句的示範。

I am writing in connection to the job advertisement. *I am writing in connection with the job advertisement.*	*1*
You will see attached CV that I have a lot of experience.	
I would like to expand I need more experience.	
I believed I am qualified.	
I would be interested to meeting you.	
I look forward to hear from you.	

Task 9 ▶參考答案

請核對寫出的正確句子和錯誤原因的編號是否如下。也可再聽一遍 MP3 中有聲版的求職信，確認各個 set-phrases 的細節部分。

I am writing in connection to the job advertisement. *I am writing in connection **with** the job advertisement.*	1
You will see attached CV that I have a lot of experience. *You will see **from my** attached CV that I have a lot of experience.*	3
I would like to expand I need more experience. *I would like to expand **my** experience.*	4
I believed I am qualified. *I **believe** I am qualified.*	2
I would be interested to meeting you. *I would be interested **in** meeting you.*	1
I look forward to hear from you. *I look forward to **hearing** from you.*	2

如果各位所寫的答案和參考答案南轅北轍的話，請重頭複習本節，並且特別注意 Task 7 中關於 set-phrases 四個細節問題點的解說。另外也可再次閱讀 Task 6 的求職信範例，參考其中 set-phrases 的用法。如有必要，請現在就回頭複習。本書的許多 Task 會幫各位將注意力集中在 set-phrases 的類似細節上，各位只須詳讀、多聽、作答和核對答案，無須擔心其背後原因。

● 本書的架構為何？

本書分成兩大部分，Part 1 專門教各位求職過程中的寫作技巧。 Unit 1 介紹的是兩種不同履歷表的寫作技巧。以職場新手凱文和職場老手黛西做例子，除了為各位示範該如何潤飾履歷表，以及如何強調應徵工作的相關經驗之外，還會為各位介紹一些實用的技巧，將潤飾和強調的手法應用在各位的履歷表上。 Unit 2 的重點則在於介紹求職信的撰寫，來襯托並凸顯各位量身訂做的履歷表。本書將會示範凱文和黛西如何在求職信中特別強調各類經驗，也會教各位一些用語以達到相同的效果。

　　本書 Part 2 的學習重點則在於求職過程中的口說能力和聽力。在 Unit 3 中將爲各位示範凱文和黛西如何準備各自領域的術語，以及與其想進入的公司相關的詞彙。在這個單元中，也將提供許多面試時會遇到的範例問題。至於 Unit 4 的焦點則放在面試時的各類狀況，提供各位實用、好用的 set-phrases，期望能讓各位在面對不同問題時，皆能應對得宜、見招拆招，此外，還提供各位一些必備且基本的聽力和發音練習。

　　除了這些單元之外，本書書末還整理出一些實用的附錄。附錄一是追蹤用的電子郵件範例，供各位在面試之後詢問後續和結果。附錄二則是本書所有的求職必備語庫一覽表，方便各位查考和參閱。

● 我該如何利用本書達到最佳學習效果？

　　以下提供若干自學秘訣，助各位一臂之力發揮最大的學習效率：

1. 本書有三種使用方法。其一，各位可以按照本書所編排的單元和順序逐一研讀；其二，各位可以根據特定求職階段，專心學習符合個別需求的單元；至於第三種方式則是在每個單元中，選擇最貼近自己現況的人物——凱文或黛西——做爲學習的範例。

2. 每個單元都會重複一些之前提過的用語或概念，用意是在加深各位對求職的各類技巧和用語的了解。因此，倘若一開始稍有不解之處，請耐心看下去，看到後面其他單元時便會自然明瞭了。

3. 研讀各單元時請不要跳過任何練習的 Task。這些 Task 有助於記憶本書的字串，亦可加強各位對這些字串的理解，所以不可輕忽。

4. 建議各位在做本書的 Task 時皆以鉛筆作答，如此，即使稍有寫錯也可擦掉再試一次。

5. 在做分類練習時，請在每個 set-phrase 旁簡單加註一個符號或字母即可。不過，建議各位稍後有空時，還是回頭將 set-phrases 抄寫在正確的欄位中。各位還記得當初是怎麼學寫中文字的嗎？沒錯！抄寫能夠加深印象。

6. 請善加利用本書所附的 MP3 光碟來輔助各位的發音和聽力練習。聽力練習永
   不嫌多。而發音練習也有助於各位背誦 set-phrases 、確認聽力，以及最重要
   的，幫助各位在面試時自信滿滿而且運用自如。

祝馬到成功，求職愉快！

Part 1

求職寫作篇

履歷表和求職信的撰寫訣竅

履歷表和求職信是各位推銷自己的工具。

履歷表的目的在於爭取到面試機會。而為了達到此目的，各位的履歷表應該要能表現出自己專業的一面，讓對方覺得值得找你面試和進一步瞭解。雖然，各國的履歷表寫法和格式不盡相同，實際上，並沒有硬性的規則可供依循。無論各位是否按照某些規則撰寫履歷表，人力資源部和進行招聘的公司主要還是會挑選他們感興趣、想加以瞭解的求職者前來面試，因此，履歷表最重要的目的應該是要「引起對方的興趣」。光靠粉紅色紙張列印出的履歷表，或是履歷表上貼的美美照片是沒有用的，而是該想辦法如何在眾多競爭對手之中，展露個人亮眼的專業能力和條件。你的履歷表即代表你本人，如果履歷表寫得讓人覺得很專業，別人也會覺得你具備專業能力，反之履歷表寫得讓人覺得不夠專業，別人也就會覺得你的專業條件不足。順帶一提的是，在美語和美國就業市場中，將履歷表稱之為 resume。然而在全世界的其他地方都稱之為 CV，全名即拉丁文的 Curriculum Vitae，是指 life course（生命歷程）的意思。為了方便起見，本書從現在起都用 CV 來稱履歷表。

至於求職信的用途，除了將 CV 中的部分資訊加以詳述，以輔助說明 CV 之外，還有補充 CV 的重要細節，以凸顯生涯和經驗中特定部分的功能。此外，CV 尚有另一個用途，那就是向對方展現自己的英文寫作能力，讓對方藉此判斷你的用字遣詞是否精準、段落組織是否簡潔，以及資訊呈現是否明確。

一般而言，CV 和求職信可分為兩大類：非目標式和目標式。有明確的理想工作時，各位可採用目標式的 CV 和求職信，針對求才廣告或徵才啓事中限定的條件撰寫。這類 CV 和求職信適用於單一讀者、單一公司、單項工作，因此，首要考量應該是表現出自己的條件和經驗是如何地符合該項工作的要求。

相較於目標式的 CV 和求職信，非目標式的內容就比較一般。這類 CV 和求職信通常是以一式寄給很多家公司，希望能遇到其中一家對自己感興趣而給予面試機會，並非專門針對某項工作而撰寫，因此，在寫這類 CV 和求職信時，應該要以多重讀者、多數公司、多重工作為考量，重點放在你個人的一般條件和經驗上。

　　不用說，通常目標式的 CV 和求職信要比非目標式的來得適當而且有效，不過在某些情況之下非目標式的 CV 和求職信也能派上用場，例如：剛開始找工作的時候、目標式的 CV 和求職信都石沉大海的時候，或是找什麼工作都無所謂只求快找到就好的時候。此外，非目標式的 CV 和求職信也適合投給人力招聘公司和企業獵才服務業者。

　　現在，我們就開始學習這些能讓各位的 CV 和求職信看起來更專業、能從眾多競爭對手當中脫穎而出的訣竅吧！這一節將從三大方向爲各位加以說明，協助各位寫出出色的 CV 和求職信。

● CV 和求職信應該讀起來一目瞭然

　　❑ 寫 CV 時以條列式逐項列出資料，文字力求精簡。這並非要各位不能寫成句子，而是應以關鍵內容的詞彙、動詞和職稱爲重，對方才能輕鬆找到你所提供的重要資料，不必仔細閱讀過多的文字。稍後在 Unit 2 將會爲各位介紹撰寫 CV 時可用上的主要動詞。

　　❑ 重要資訊可用粗體字或不同大小的字型凸顯，但需注意閱覽時的整體感。不要穿插過多不同大小的字型，以免顯得凌亂失焦，兩種應該就綽綽有餘了。

　　❑ 把所有的資訊集中放在一頁之內。人力資源部瀏覽 CV 時幾乎不會翻頁看到下一頁。所以，如果履歷很長，無法在一頁之內描述完，還是務請精挑和細選資訊。

　　❑ 爲免隨 CV 所附的求職信遺失，記得在 CV 中也要附上姓名、出生年月日、國籍和所有聯絡方式。至於身分證或護照號碼則不必註明。

● 讓 CV 和求職信看起來吸引人

　　❑ 使用看起來專業的字體。建議各位用 Arial、Verdana 和 Times New Roman 這三種商務上最常使用的字體，看起來也最專業。

　　❑ 勿把資訊擠在一起。每頁的邊界要夠寬，CV 和求職信才會讓人讀起來舒服順暢，視覺上沒有侷促感。

❑ 如果要把 CV 和求職信列印出來用郵寄或遞交的話，可以採用稍微有一點厚度、品質較高的 A4 紙張，紙張顏色則可挑選略帶灰色或黃色，如乳白色、米色或淺灰色等。當 CV 和求職信摸起來質感良好、看起來賞心悅目時，相信人力資源部和招聘公司的人員也會對你的專業度留下好感，進而給予面試機會。

❑ 如果有專業形象的近照也可以附在 CV 上，不過這點並非必要。假使照片所佔空間太大則可省略不附。

● 對細節一絲不苟

❑ 一而再、再而三地檢查拼字、用字和標點符號的正確度。CV 和求職信中出現打錯或拼錯的字是不可原諒的。如果換做是你在應徵者的 CV 和求職信中看到拼錯的字，你應該也不會僱用他吧？

❑ 標點符號、定位點和行距要上下一致。必須一而再、再而三地校對，至於求職信中的文法和用字，更需花工夫仔細審閱。

❑ 檢查所有日期。一個無心的小錯誤可能就會讓你的履歷留下一段空白經歷，對方看到可能會納悶你在某年中有三個月在做什麼，搞不好是在吃牢飯呢？

❑ 不要撒謊。如果你有一段時間失業或因其他某種因素沒有工作，別在 CV 或求職信中不打自招，不過得做好萬全準備，在面試時對方可能會問起。人力資源部和招聘公司會注意到你 CV 中的空窗期，但不要編造出你在屏東幫叔叔工作之類的謊話來搪塞。

❑ 寄出 CV 或求職信之前，可以先請別人幫你校對錯別字、格式的連貫性和日期等。

Unit ①

履歷表
The CV / Resume

 # 引言與學習目標

在本單元中我們要學的是撰寫非目標式（untargeted）和目標式（targeted）的 CV，本單元學習結束之前，各位應該達成的學習目標如下：

- ❏ 學到一些一般訣竅，懂得如何寫出專業的 CV。
- ❏ 知道在 CV 中應該提供何種資訊以及呈現資訊的方法。
- ❏ 理解目標式和非目標式 CV 之間的差異，以及撰寫目標式 CV 時的考量。
- ❏ 能夠針對特定的求才廣告量身訂做 CV，並在 CV 中詳述相關經驗。
- ❏ 學會在 CV 的個人簡介（profile）中重複運用求才廣告上的詞彙，寫出更切合雇主要求的簡介。
- ❏ 能夠針對不同的求才廣告撰寫個人簡介。
- ❏ 學會運用各種形容詞來描述自己所具備的技能和條件。
- ❏ 學到一些個人簡介會用到的 chunks。
- ❏ 做過個人簡介和 CV 寫作的練習。

非目標式 CV

我們來看一下凱文和黛西的非目標式 CV，以便了解他們的工作資歷。

Task **1.1**

請研究下面兩份非目標式 CV 有何不同和相同之處？

非目標式 CV ：職場新手篇

KEVIN GAO	
Telephone: 0912 345 678	Email: Kevin11@notmail.com
Date of Birth: 1985/05/06	Nationality: Taiwanese

PROFILE

A promising[1] business administration major with a strong interest in marketing, sales, and logistics.[2] Excellent academic results in all areas. Thesis topic: "The Importance of Marketing Strategies in The Greater China Market." Firsthand work experience in marketing, sales, administration, and PR related activities in a variety of different segments. Strong computer and interpersonal skills, and experience with financial management.

EDUCATION

2003 - 2007	BA, Business Administration, Hao Li Hai (HLH) University, Taiwan.
2001 - 2003	Second Lieutenant, ROC Marine Corps, Penghu, Taiwan
1998 - 2001	Diploma, Zui Hao High School, Taipei

Word List

1 promising [ˈprɑmɪsɪŋ] *adj.* 有前景的
2 logistics [loˈdʒɪstɪks] *n.* 物流

WORK EXPERIENCE

2007 Winter	Part time temp in marketing department, Taipei 101
	▶ Planned and implemented[3] anniversary event
2006 Summer	Temporary sales clerk at Campho Ltd.
	▶ Sold photographic equipment to wholesale overseas buyers
2006 Winter	Stock control clerk at Costco
	▶ Assisted in wholesale stock control
2005 Summer	Sales clerk in 7-Eleven store
	▶ Managed in-store[4] inventory controls
2005 Winter	Sales clerk in 7-Eleven store
	▶ Operated cash register and dealt with customers
2004 Summer	Telemarketing[5] clerk at Hai Hao La Buxiban
	▶ Focused on sales
2004 Winter	Inquiries clerk at Hai Hao La Buxiban
	▶ Focused on incoming inquiries[6]

OTHER ACTIVITIES

2005 - 2007	Treasurer[7] of HLH University Photographer's Association
	▶ Managed club bank accounts and treasury
2004 - 2005	English camp counselor, HLH University

RELEVANT SKILLS

English (GEPT Upper Intermediate)

Computer skills: Excel, Word, PowerPoint, FrontPage

Competent driver with valid license

HOBBIES AND INTERESTS

Photography, swimming, reading, music

Word List

3 implement [ˈɪmpləˌmɛnt] *v.* 實行
4 in-store [ɪnˈstor] *adj.* 倉庫內的
5 telemarketing [ˌtɛləˈmɑrkɪtɪŋ] *n.* 電話行銷
6 inquiries [ɪnˈkwaɪrɪ] *n.* 詢問
7 treasurer [ˈtrɛʒərə] *n.* 出納

高凱文	
電話： 0912 345 678	電子信箱：Kevin11@notmail.com
出生日期：1985/05/06	國籍：台灣

個人簡介

　　主修商業管理，前途可爲，對行銷、業務和物流有濃厚興趣。在校各科成績優異。畢業論文以「大中華市場中行銷策略的重要性」爲題。在各個不同領域均有第一手的行銷、售貨、行政、公關等工作經驗。電腦技能強，人際關係好，具備財務管理的經驗。

教育程度

2003 - 2007	台灣好厲害大學企業管理學士
2001 - 2003	澎湖海軍陸戰隊二等中尉
1998 - 2001	台北最好高中

工作經驗

2007 冬	台北 101 行銷部兼職工讀生
	▶ 計畫與執行週年慶節目
2006 夏	Campho 臨時售貨員
	▶ 對國外批發商銷售攝影設備
2006 冬	好市多庫存管理員
	▶ 協助批發庫存的控管
2005 夏	7-Eleven 商店售貨員
	▶ 管理店內存貨
2005 冬	7-Eleven 商店售貨員
	▶ 收銀與消費者服務
2004 夏	還好拉補習班電話行銷員
	▶ 主要負責業務
2004 冬	還好拉補習班客戶服務員
	▶ 專門處裡客戶詢問

其他活動
2005 - 2007　好厲害大學攝影社財務股長 　　　　　　　▶ 管理社團銀行帳戶和財務 2004 - 2005　好厲害大學英文營輔導員
相關技能
英文（全民英檢中高級程度） 電腦技能：Excel 、 Word 、 PowerPoint 、 FrontPage 汽車駕照
嗜好及興趣
攝影、游泳、閱讀、音樂

非目標式 CV：職場老手篇

DAISY WANG	
Telephone: 0987 654 321	Email: Daisy.Wang@notmail.com
Date of Birth: 1970/05/06	Nationality: Taiwanese

PROFILE

An experienced finance professional with excellent academic qualifications. A Certified Public Accountant (ROC) and ACCA member with know-how in public accounting, managing finances and tax returns for local companies. Experience with corporate client service management in an international auditing company, and managing international clients' relations with local tax authorities. Recent special emphasis on offshore tax environments. Currently in final stage of part-time MBA focusing on international tax law.

EDUCATION

2006 - present	MBA (part time) program, Nemme Hao University, Taiwan
2000	ACCA, Leicester University, UK
1994 - 1997	BA, Business Administration, Fei Chang Hao University, Taiwan

WORK EXPERIENCE

2005 - present	Client service Manager, KPGM, Taiwan
	▸ Manage three major international corporate clients
	▸ Have overall responsibility for clients' ROC tax affairs
	▸ Increase clients' tax savings by utilizing international tax environments
2003 - 2005	Assistant Manager, Finance Department, BonK Inc., Taiwan
	▸ Oversaw audits for all subsidiaries[1]
	▸ Carried out annual tax audit
	▸ Responsible for synchronization[2] of tax affairs during merger
	▸ Advised on legal taxation issues

Word List

1 subsidiary [səbˋsɪdɪˌɛrɪ] *n.* 子公司
2 synchronization [ˌsɪŋkrənɪˋzeʃən] *n.* 同時性，校準

2001 - 2003	Senior Auditor, Hao Bu Hao Plastics Corporation, Taiwan
	▶ Managed team of finance personnel
	▶ Set up new financial reporting systems to facilitate EOY[3] accounts
1997 - 2000	Accountant Clerk, Sunshine Certified Public Accountants, Taiwan
	▶ Carried out annual tax audits for local small-to-medium sized companies

RELEVANT SKILLS

Fluent in Mandarin, Cantonese and English

Computer skills: Excel, Word, PowerPoint, FrontPage, Kerridge Systems, Reuters

Word List   3 EOY = end of year 年底

王黛西	
電話： 0987 654 321	電子郵件： Daisy.Wang@notmail.com
出生日期： 1970/05/06	國籍：台灣

個人簡介

　　經驗豐富的財務專業人才，教育背景優異。持有會計師執照（中華民國）並為國際認可的特許公認會計師會員，具有公開發行會計、財務管理和為本地公司結算申報的實務經驗。具有在國際會計師事務所中管理企業客戶服務的經驗，亦曾為國際客戶處理與本地政府稅務機關之間的關係。近來工作重點則在境外稅務環境。目前在職攻讀商管碩士學位已到最後一個階段，主修國際稅法。

教育程度

2006 - 目前	台灣那麼好大學商管碩士（在職生）
2000	英國萊斯特大學國際公認特許會計師文憑
1994 - 1997	台灣非常好大學企業管理學士

工作經驗

2005 - 目前	台灣 KPGM 客戶服務經理
	▶ 負責三個主要國際企業客戶
	▶ 全權負責客戶在中華民國的稅務
	▶ 利用國際稅務環境為客戶增加節稅
2003 - 2005	台灣 BonK 財務部副理
	▶ 監督所有子公司的查帳審核事務
	▶ 執行年度稅務審查
	▶ 在公司合併過程中整合稅務
	▶ 針對稅法議題提供建議
2001 - 2003	台灣好不好塑膠公司資深審計員
	▶ 負責領導一組財務人員工作團隊
	▶ 建立新的財務報告系統，輔助年終帳戶結算
1997 - 2000	台灣陽光執業會計師事務所會計雇員
	▶ 為本地中小型企業做年度稅務查帳審核

相關專長

國語、廣東話、英文流利

電腦技能：Excel、Word、PowerPoint、Front Page、Kerridge Systems、Reuters

Task 1.1 ▶參考答案

我們來看一下這兩份 CV 之間的相同和不同之處。

相同處

▶ 這兩份 CV 都是從姓名和個人資料開始寫起,並包括聯絡方式。

▶ 然後寫的是個人簡介(profile)。個人簡介的用處在於簡述你的個人條件,也給對方一個機會瞭解你對自己的看法。這兩位求職者的個人簡介均少於 100字。本單元稍後將為各位介紹個人簡介的寫法。

▶ 接著將 CV 劃分為三大段:學歷(Education)、工作經驗(Work Experience)和相關技能(Relevant Skills)。

▶ 在工作經驗這一段中,應該將最近或目前所從事的工作寫在最前面。對雇主來說你目前在做什麼要比你在十年前做了什麼來得重要。

▶ 每份工作的敘述都應該從職稱寫起,接著是公司名稱和公司所在地。主要工作項目敘述完之後,下方再以條列式逐項用主動動詞(active verbs)描述實際的職務內容。每一項職務都以動詞開頭,不需使用主詞(只有 responsible for 例外,不僅主詞不用出現,也不要用 be 動詞開頭)。

▶ 列出目前的工作時,動詞時態應該要用現在簡單式,至於過去的工作則要用過去簡單式。 CV 中只要用這兩種動詞時態即可,下一單元將介紹動詞時態的運用。

▶ 日期要以國際通用的西元格式清楚置於左方,而非以中文格式(民國)書寫。

▶ 整份 CV 的內文中,除了個人簡介以外,沒有用到完整的句子,而且文字也很精簡。動詞都沒有主詞。內文的重點則擺在和職稱、職務有關的字詞。這種寫法可以幫助審閱 CV 的雇主迅速而有效率地找到所需的資料,亦即只需快速瀏覽內文找到重要資訊,而不需逐字詳讀。

▶ 這兩份 CV 從頭到尾只用了二到三種不同大小的字體,因此讀起來簡單大方。邊寬也恰到好處,並沒有將各項資訊擠在一處。

▶ 內文都沒有提到求職者的家庭背景。通常西方公司的雇主對你的家庭背景不感興趣,因此在國際公司求職時,英文 CV 和求職信中不需提供這類資訊。

不同處

▶ 各位可能注意到的第一個不同處，就是凱文的 CV 竟然比黛西的長。這是因為凱文做過的短期兼職工作比黛西多。雖然黛西服務過的公司較少，但是每一份工作的任職時間都較長。

▶ 此外，各位可能注意到的第二個不同處，就是凱文的 CV 是從學歷開始寫起，而黛西的則從工作經驗寫起。這是由於黛西比凱文年長、經驗也較為豐富，而且待在就業市場上的時間也較長的緣故。對審閱 CV 的雇主而言，她的工作經驗會比學歷來得重要。反觀凱文，他的經驗不多而且還是學生身分，因此他把學歷寫在前面，主要強調自己大學和高中的背景。雇主並不想知道從國中以降到幼稚園的這些背景。

▶ 凱文在日期旁邊標明季節，表示這些是在學校放假時的打工，而黛西則只有寫出年份。月份則不需標明，通常這算是枝微末節，更何況有時根本記不清楚自己是幾月開始上班、幾月離職的。

▶ 凱文的動詞全部都用過去式，因為他現在沒有在上班。黛西工作經驗的第一筆資料則是用動詞現在簡單式，因為她所描述的是目前的職務。

▶ 凱文在 CV 中提到了其他活動（Other Activities），因為他的工作資歷不是很深。他希望凸顯他在大學社團所得到的一些經驗也可運用在商業職場中。

▶ 凱文在 CV 中納入了嗜好和興趣（Hobbies and Interests），因為他還年輕，雇主會希望了解他的個性。黛西沒有附上這些資料，因為她已經是專業人士，就現階段的人生或事業而言，她的嗜好和興趣並非重點。

即使不了解凱文和黛西在撰寫 CV 時的背後考量，也希望各位至少能看出兩者之間所有的相同和不同之處。

Task 1.2

請撰寫並閱讀自己的非目標式 CV ，根據以上所學做適當的修改。書末附有空白的履歷表格式供各位利用。

 # 目標式 CV

現在就讓我們來學習如何針對某項特定工作，改寫非目標式 CV 中的基本資料，希望能藉此爭取到面試機會。就先從凱文的開始吧，他看到兩則不同的求才廣告，兩份工作他都感興趣，也都想應徵看看。

Task 1.3

請閱讀下面第一則求才廣告。以各位對凱文學歷和資歷的了解，你覺得他為什麼會對這份工作感興趣？

● 求才廣告 I

Expressways Resin
Sales and Logistics Personnel Wanted

Expressways Resin is a growing international plastics and rubber distribution business that is part of a pan-[1]Asian network of sister companies. We are the leading thermoplastic raw material distributor in Asia, and our customers and suppliers represent China's leading blue chip[2] manufacturers. We are an owned subsidiary of Taiwan Plastics Company, Inc.

We have positions available in both our sales and logistics departments. We seek ambitious, team-orientated, university graduates to join a dynamic, growing company. Successful candidates will need to have a business degree, be interested in technical sales, and have some sales and marketing experience. Interest in—or past experience with—inventory management is a plus.

We desire applicants who are motivated by the challenge of constantly learning new skills in all aspects of the business, and who are excited by opportunities for career development. Our compensation package is among the best in the industry and reflects our commitment to nurturing talent.

Successful candidates will undergo[3] an individual training and development program, personalized to reflect his or her needs. These programs are designed to provide the necessary skills and knowledge to excel in the position. Training and development needs will be discussed at regular reviews.

Please send a cover letter and CV to: Nancy_Drew@anemailaddresslikethis.net

● **內容摘要**

> **Expressways Resin**
> **誠徵業務與物流人員**
>
> Expressways Resin 為一快速成長中的國際塑膠暨橡膠批發公司，在泛亞網絡中尚有許多姐妹公司。我們是亞洲的熱塑性原料領導者，客戶和供應商亦為中國頂尖的藍籌股製造業者，而且是台灣塑膠公司的子公司。
>
> 我們的業務部和物流部均有空缺，徵求有上進心、喜歡團隊工作的畢業生加入我們充滿活力、不斷成長的公司。應徵者需具備商學學位、對技術性業務有興趣，有售貨和行銷的經驗而且對庫存管理也有經驗和興趣。
>
> 應徵者需喜歡接受挑戰，不斷學習工作上所有層面的新技能，並且有興趣利用機會發展事業。薪酬待遇為業界之最，因而反映出我們對培養人才的執著。
>
> 應徵成功者將接受個別訓練和上發展課程，兩者均根據個別需求而設計。這些課程的目的在於為新進者準備因應工作所需的技能和知識。我們會定期召開審查會，討論個人的培訓和發展需求。
>
> 意者請將求職信和 CV 寄至： Nancy_Drew@anemailaddresslikethis.net

Task **1.3** ▶ 參考答案

　　各位可能會覺得凱文對這份工作的薪水和福利感興趣，此外，受訓機會一定也很吸引他。不過凱文自知資歷尚淺，就現階段的他而言，應找尋的是符合自己技能和經歷的工作，而非打從一開始就往理想工作方面尋找，如此才容易過關斬將爭取到面試機會。

　　這份工作或許符合凱文的期望，因為它的工作內容和售貨有關，而凱文正好在 7-Eleven 和 Campho 打工時期獲得了一些售貨經驗。他在好市多（Costco）打工時也接觸過一些物流經驗。Expressways Resin 的市場在中國，而凱文的論文恰好寫的就是大中華市場的行銷。所以他認為這些資歷對 Expressways Resin 的人資部來說，將會把他列入理想人選。

　　現在我們來看一看凱文感興趣的另一份工作。

Word List   1 pan- [pæn-] *adj.* 總，泛   3 undergo [ˌʌndəˋgo] *v.* 接受
               2 blue chip *n.* 績優股

Task 1.4

　　請閱讀下面這第二則求才廣告。以各位對凱文學歷和資歷的了解，你覺得他為什麼會對這份工作感興趣？

● 求才廣告 II

> ### Clerks
> ### Trade Fair Event Trainee Manager
>
> 　　We are one of the world's largest, non-athletic shoe brands and boast[1] outlets, sourcing[2] operations, factories, and customers in every continent. We have one hundred eighty years of shoemaking history behind us and are constantly developing and employing new and innovative ways of manufacturing and selling shoes. Our fastest growing market is China and the Asia-Pacific Region.
>
> 　　We seek a Trade Fair Event Trainee Manager to assist in marketing event management. This includes the setting up, running, and taking down of our booths at international and regional trade fairs. The successful applicant will be expected to provide creative input into the design of the booth in accordance with our corporate image and goals, and also to participate in sales, managing customer inquiries, and handling large orders made at the fair. In addition, the successful candidate will be responsible for event budget management.
>
> 　　The position offers a generous remuneration[3] package and lots of opportunities for international travel. Training will be provided. Excellent potential for advancement.[4]
>
> 　　Please send a cover letter and CV to: Bill_Sikes@anemailaddresslikethis.net

Word List

1 boast [bost] v. 以擁有…而自豪
2 source [sors] v. 開源
3 remuneration [rɪ͵mjunəˋreʃən] n. 酬勞
4 advancement [ədˋvænsmənt] n. 晉升

● 內容摘要

Clerks
商展活動培訓主管

　　本公司為世界屬一屬二的（非運動）鞋子品牌，擁有暢貨店、採購營運中心、工廠，客戶遍及各大洲。我們擁有 180 年的製鞋歷史，但仍持續不斷地研發和採用嶄新而富有創意的製鞋和行銷方法。我們成長最快的市場即為中國和亞太地區。

　　本公司徵求商展活動培訓主管一名，協助行銷活動的管理，職務內容包括在國際和地區性商展中搭建、經營和拆卸攤位。應徵成功者將根據本企業的形象和目標，為攤位的設計貢獻其創意，並在展期中參與業務、處理客戶詢問和大宗訂單。除此之外，應徵成功者也將負責管理活動預算。

　　薪酬待遇優，出國機會多。提供培訓，升遷機會高。

　　意者請將求職信和履歷寄至：Bill_Sikes@anemailaddresslikethis.net

Task 1.4 ▶參考答案

　　同樣地，各位可能覺得凱文是對升遷機會高感興趣，還可以到國外許多有趣的地方出差和認識很多新朋友。這或許是他考慮應徵這份工作的原因之一，不過他為了提高勝出的機會，同時也考慮到他自己的專長和經歷是否符合條件。

　　他在寒假時曾經在台北 101 打工，得到一些活動管理的經驗；他的論文是以行銷為題；他在學校放假時找到的第一份工作也與處理客戶詢問有關，不論批發或零售方面都有售貨的經驗；此外，他在大學攝影社當過財務股長，對預算管理不無了解。他認為對 Clerks 的人資部來說，這些資歷都會讓他成為該項職務的理想人選。

　　現在我們來看一看凱文如何修改非目標式 CV，以凸顯他的資歷符合這兩則求才廣告的要求條件。

目標式 CV 1：職場新手篇

KEVIN GAO	
Telephone: 0912 345 678	Email: Kevin11@notmail.com
Date of Birth: 1985/05/06	Nationality: Taiwanese

PROFILE

A promising business administration major with a strong interest in marketing and event management. Excellent academic results in all areas. Thesis topic: "The Importance of Marketing Strategies in The Greater China Market." Firsthand work experience in marketing event management and PR related activities—from design to execution[1]—and managing customer inquiries. Strong interpersonal skills and substantial[2] experience with budget[3] management.

POSITION

Trade Fair Event Trainee Manager

EDUCATION

2003 - 2007	BA, Business Administration, Hao Li Hai (HLH) University, Taiwan
2001 - 2003	Second Lieutenant, ROC Marine Corps, Penghu, Taiwan
1998 - 2001	Diploma, Zui Hao High School, Taipei

WORK EXPERIENCE

2007 Winter	Part time temp in marketing department, Taipei 101

- ▶ Planned anniversary event according to brief
- ▶ Worked on all stages of project, from inception,[4] to setting up and inquiries
- ▶ Had special responsibility for designing and distributing flyers and DMs

Word List

1 execution [ˌɛksɪˈkjuʃən] *n.* 執行　　3 budget [ˈbʌdʒɪt] *n.* 預算

2 substantial [səbˈstænʃəl] *adj.* 可觀的　4 inception [ɪnˈsɛpʃən] *n.* 開端

2006 Summer	Temporary sales clerk at Campho Ltd.
	▸ Sold photographic equipment to wholesale overseas buyers
	▸ Dealt with customer inquiries
	▸ Handled bulk orders, from initial inquiry to collection and shipping
2006 Winter	Stock control clerk at Costco
2005 Summer	Senior sales clerk in 7-Eleven store
	▸ Operated cash register and dealt with customers
	▸ Managed team of three junior clerks
2005 Winter	Sales clerk in 7-Eleven store
2004 Summer	Telemarketing clerk at Hai Hao La Buxiban
	▸ Achieved highest summer sales targets
2004 Winter	Telemarketing clerk at Hai Hao La Buxiban
	▸ Handled incoming inquiries
	▸ Responsible for matching students with appropriate courses

OTHER ACTIVITIES

2005 - 2007	Treasurer of HLH University Photographers Association
	▸ Responsible for collecting membership dues[5]
	▸ Managed budgets for events and activities
	▸ Increased club revenues by 34 percent during second year
2004 - 2005	English camp counselor, HLH University

RELEVANT SKILLS

English (GEPT Upper Intermediate)

Computer skills: Excel, Word, PowerPoint, FrontPage, and Dreamweaver

Competent driver with valid license

HOBBIES AND INTERESTS

Photography, design, swimming, reading, music

Word List　5 due [dju] *n.* 會費

高凱文	
電話： 0912 345 678	電子信箱：Kevin11@notmail.com
出生日期：1985/05/06	國籍：台灣

個人簡介

　　主修商業管理，前途可為，對行銷和活動管理有濃厚興趣。在校各科成績優異。畢業論文以「大中華市場中行銷策略的重要性」為題。從設計、執行到處理客戶詢問，具有行銷活動管理和公關方面的第一手工作經驗。人際關係好，具有預算管理的經驗。

應徵職位

商展活動培訓主管

教育程度

2003 - 2007	台灣好厲害大學企業管理學士
2001 - 2003	澎湖海軍陸戰隊二等中尉
1998 - 2001	台北最好高中

工作經驗

2007 冬　　　台北 101 行銷部兼職工讀生
- ▶ 根據概要計畫週年慶節目
- ▶ 從發想、建立到客戶詢問，全程參與計畫的所有階段
- ▶ 特別負責設計和分發傳單和 DM

2006 夏　　　Campho 臨時售貨員
- ▶ 對國外批發商銷售攝影設備
- ▶ 處理客戶詢問
- ▶ 處理大宗訂單，始自前端的詢問到後端的收貨和運寄

2006 冬　　　好市多存貨管理員

2005 夏　　　7-Eleven 商店資深售貨員
- ▶ 收銀與消費者服務
- ▶ 領導一組工作團隊，其中共有三名新進售貨員

2005 冬　　　7-Eleven 商店售貨員

2004 夏	還好拉補習班電話行銷員
	▸ 達到暑期業務最高目標
2004 冬	還好拉補習班電話行銷員
	▸ 專門處裡客戶詢問
	▸ 負責將學生分配到適當的班級

其他活動

2005 - 2007	好厲害大學攝影社財務股長
	▸ 負責收取會費
	▸ 管理節目和活動預算
	▸ 在第二年爲社團增加了三成四的收入
2004 - 2005	好厲害大學英文營輔導員

相關技能

英文（全民英檢中高級程度）
電腦技能：Excel 、 Word 、 PowerPoint 、 FrontPage 、 Dreamweaver
汽車駕照

嗜好及興趣

攝影、設計、游泳、閱讀、音樂

目標式 CV 2：職場新手篇

KEVIN GAO	
Telephone: 0912 345 678	Email: Kevin11@notmail.com
Date of Birth: 1985/05/06	Nationality: Taiwanese

PROFILE

A promising business administration major with a strong interest in logistics and sales. Excellent academic results in all areas. Thesis topic: "The Importance of Marketing Strategies in The Greater China Market." Firsthand work experience of logistics and sales in both technical and FMCG[1] segments. Excellent track record[2] in inventory management and warehouse improvement.

POSITION

Sales and Logistics

EDUCATION

2003 - 2007	BA, Business Administration, Hao Li Hai (HLH) University, Taiwan
2001 - 2003	Second Lieutenant, ROC Marine Corps, Penghu, Taiwan
1998 - 2001	Diploma, Zui Hao High School, Taipei

WORK EXPERIENCE

2007 Winter	Part time temp, Marketing Department, Taipei 101
2006 Summer	Temporary sales clerk at Campho Ltd.

- ▸ Sold photographic equipment to wholesale overseas buyers
- ▸ Responsible for matching new products with customer needs
- ▸ Brought in two major new customers through contacts with college Photographers Association
- ▸ Responsible for maintaining good customer relations with after sales service

Word List

1 FMCG = Fast Moving Consumer Goods 消費性產品
2 track record *n.* 成績，業績

2006 Winter	Stock control clerk at Costco
	▸ Assisted in wholesale stock control
	▸ Managed green goods inventory and warehouse
	▸ Kept up inventory during the very busy Chinese New Year period
	▸ Developed and maintained relations with new suppliers
2005 Summer	Sales clerk in 7-Eleven store
	▸ Upgraded and improved in-store inventory controls
	▸ Trained new sales in the improved system
	▸ Reorganized storage room to create new space to assist in stock management
2005 Winter	Sales clerk in 7-Eleven store
2004 Summer	Telemarketing clerk at Hai Hao La Buxiban
	▸ Achieved highest summer sales targets
2004 Winter	Telemarketing clerk at Hai Hao La Buxiban

OTHER ACTIVITIES

2005 - 2007	Treasurer of HLH University Photographers Association

RELEVANT SKILLS

English (GEPT Upper Intermediate)

Computer skills: Excel, Word, PowerPoint, FrontPage

Competent driver with valid license

HOBBIES AND INTERESTS

Photography, swimming, reading, music

高凱文	
電話： 0912 345 678	電子信箱： Kevin11@notmail.com
出生日期： 1985/05/06	國籍：台灣

自傳

　　主修商業管理，前途可爲，對物流和業務有濃厚興趣。在校各科成績優異。畢業論文以「大中華市場中行銷策略的重要性」爲題。在技術和快速流通消費部門均有第一手的物流和售貨經驗。在存貨管理和倉庫改善方面的業績卓越。

應徵職位

業務和物流

教育程度

2003 - 2007	台灣好厲害大學企業管理學士
2001 - 2003	澎湖海軍陸戰隊二等中尉
1998 - 2001	台北最好高中

工作經驗

2007 冬　　台北 101 行銷部兼職工讀生

2006 夏　　Campho 臨時售貨員

　▶ 對國外批發商銷售攝影設備
　▶ 負責根據客戶需求推薦新產品
　▶ 透過在大學攝影社的人脈爲公司帶來兩名新的重要客戶
　▶ 負責售後服務，與客戶維持良好的關係

2006 冬　　好市多存貨管理員

　▶ 協助批發的存貨控管
　▶ 管理綠色產品的存貨和倉儲
　▶ 在忙碌的春節期間維持存貨水準
　▶ 與新供應商建立並維持關係

2005 夏	**7-Eleven** 商店售貨員
	▸ 升級和改善店內存貨控管系統
	▸ 訓練新進售貨員運用改善後的系統
	▸ 重新整理倉庫，挪出新空間以改善存貨管理
2005 冬	**7-Eleven** 商店售貨員
2004 夏	還好拉補習班電話行銷員
	▸ 達到暑期最高業務目標
2004 冬	還好拉補習班電話行銷員

其他活動

2005 - 2007	好厲害大學攝影社財務股長

相關技能

英文（全民英檢中高級程度）
電腦技能： Excel 、 Word 、 PowerPoint 、 FrontPage
汽車駕照

嗜好及興趣

攝影、游泳、閱讀、音樂

Task 1.5

請閱讀前面兩份 CV ，找出所對應的求才廣告，並將 CV 號碼寫在下表右欄。

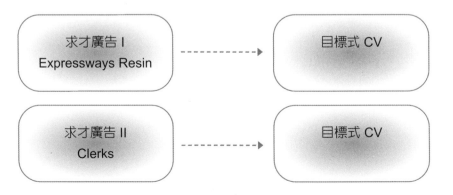

Task **1.5** ▶參考答案

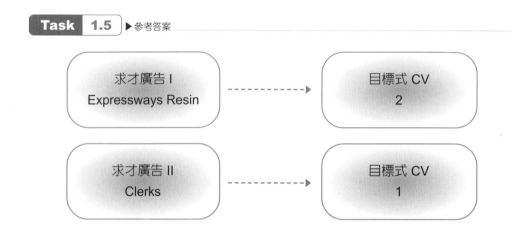

Task **1.6**

　　請仔細研讀這兩份 CV。兩者和凱文原本的非目標式 CV 之間有何相同和不同之處？凱文如何針對求才廣告設定的條件修改 CV 中的資料？

Task **1.6** ▶參考答案

　　凱文根據求才廣告要求的條件修改了 CV，希望吸引雇主注意自己符合職務要求的經驗。為達此目的，凱文在 CV 中某些部分增加好幾筆資訊加以闡述，同時刪除了非目標式 CV 中原有的幾筆資料，以免 CV 看起來太過擁擠，同時讓所欲點出的資料看起來更加顯眼和清楚。他針對求才廣告的條件，把兩份 CV 中的個人簡介也稍微修改了一下。值得注意的是，這兩份 CV 的用字遣詞依然是以簡明扼要的詞彙為重點。

　　在 CV 附帶的求職信中，凱文會擴大補充其經歷，以說明自己從相關經驗中得到些什麼收穫。這個技巧將在下一單元為各位介紹。

　　現在先來分別更進一步研究凱文的這兩份目標式 CV。

目標式 CV1

▶ 凱文在個人簡介中強調他在 101 的活動管理經驗、大學攝影社的預算管理經驗，及面對客戶的人際關係能力。他希望這些經驗和能力能夠引人注意。

▶ 凱文在 CV 上方註明了應徵職位。請不要在非目標式 CV 中註明應徵職位，以免自我設限、錯過一些機會。但請注意所有的目標式 CV 中，如何註明所欲應徵的職位。此外，他在嗜好與興趣部分增加了對設計的興趣。

▶ 在 CV 的主體部分，他詳加說明了在 101 兼職時的工作內容，以示他具備活動管理的經驗。他更強調自己是全方位型的人才，活動案中所有階段的工作都有參與，包括設計宣傳單。

▶ 他也補充說明了在 Campho 上班時的職務內容，並將重點擺在行政能力和客戶關係能力之上，因為他認為這些能力和條件可以吸引雇主的青睞。

▶ 其它經驗因為與 Clerks 的資歷條件無關，他便刪掉了一些，沒有多加說明在好市多和在 7-Eleven 初次打工的經驗。在 7-Eleven 第二次打工的經驗中，他將焦點放在團隊管理的技能上，以證明他在人際關係、處理詢問和追蹤後續的能力。他認為 Clerks 的工作會需要這方面的長才。

▶ 他說明了在大學攝影社的職務，以管理預算為重點，不僅舉出他對提高收入的貢獻，更利用數據來量化業績。如果能夠取得數據，則可採用他這個做法。

目標式 CV2

▶ 在個人簡介中，凱文特別強調他在不同部門所獲得的售貨和物流、進貨控管和改善存貨盤點等經驗，因為他認為這些經驗能符合雇主的期望。

▶ 在 CV 的主體部分，他詳述了 Campho 的工作內容，顯示出他在技術部門得到的批發售貨經驗。更舉出一個具體範例，說明自己是如何增加公司的客戶群。他覺得藉此可向雇主證明自己的進取心和對公司的價值。

▶ 他詳述好市多的工作內容，特別是物流方面的技能，並具體舉出業績。

▶ 在 7-Eleven 的第二次工作資歷中，他特別強調了在提高店內儲藏空間效率方面的成就。同樣地，他希望藉此顯示出他的主動積極，以及能幫雇用公司增加財富和節省成本。

既然我們已經了解凱文如何針對求才廣告修改他的非目標式 CV，現在輪到研究黛西修改 CV 的方法了。

Task 1.7

請閱讀下面這第三則求才廣告。以你對黛西經驗和事業目標的了解，你覺得她為什麼會對這個職位感興趣？

● 求才廣告 III

Jarndyce & Jarndyce
International Tax Specialist

Hong Kong member firm of an international conglomerate[1] that is the world's second largest accountancy[2] network and boasts more than six hundred offices in one hundred countries. In Hong Kong and China, we employ more than 2,800 people across sixteen locations.

The team you will join specializes in advising individuals and corporations on high-level tax solutions. This includes advising on employer contributions, corporation tax in respect to capital gains, inheritance, and stamp duty land tax. The work involves developing tax solutions — some of which will be bespoke[3] arrangements for a particular client, and some of which will involve adapting international tax planning techniques to meet client needs.

We require a CPA and/or ACCA qualified or equivalent accountant who is able to work well in a team environment and communicate effectively with clients and staff. You will:

▸ Have experience in advising owner managed and/or entrepreneurial[4] businesses as well as some high net worth individuals, including advisory and consultancy work.
▸ Have exposure to international tax planning primarily involving taxes other than VAT.
▸ Be able to develop excellent client relations and relationships within the firm.
▸ Be able to supervise and develop staff at the supervisor level and below.
▸ Provide an efficient and proactive[5] service to clients and ensure clients' needs are fully met.
▸ Be keen to learn and develop your technical skills and have the ability to manage workloads under time pressure.

Accommodation and expenses provided. Excellent compensation package with opportunity for large performance bonuses. Must be able to relocate to Hong Kong.

Please send a cover letter and CV to: Calista_Chen@anemailaddresslikethis.net

---

Word List

1 conglomerate [kən`glɑmərɪt] *n.* 綜合企業

2 accountancy [ə`kauntənsɪ] *n.* 會計師事務

3 bespoke [bɪ`spok] *adj.* 定製的

4 entrepreneurial [ˌɑntrəprə`njurɪəl] *adj.* 企業家的

5 proactive [pro`æktɪv] *adj.* 積極的

● 內容摘要

Jarndyce & Jarndyce
國際稅務專員

　　本事務所為一國際企業集團的香港分所。本國際企業集團為世界第二大會計師事務所集團，在 100 個國家中有 600 個辦公室。本集團在香港和中國共有 16 個分所，僱用了超過 2,800 名員工。

　　您將服務的工作團隊是專門為個人和企業提供高所得的報稅諮詢服務，包括建議雇主供款、資本利得方面的公司稅、遺產稅、印花稅和土地稅。您的職務內容包括提供報稅服務，其中部分是針對特定客戶量身訂做的服務，部分則將透過國際稅務規劃的管道滿足客戶需求。

　　我們徵求合格會計師一名，亦或具備國際公認會計資格或同等學力的會計師，需善於團隊工作，並與客戶和員工溝通良好。條件如下：

▶ 有建議業主或公司企業以及一些高所得個人客戶的經驗，包括提供諮詢和顧問服務。

▶ 接觸過增值稅以外的各項國際稅務規劃。

▶ 有能力建立良好的客戶關係以及在事務所內的關係。

▶ 有能力監督和建立主管級以下的員工群。

▶ 為客戶提供高效率和積極的服務，確實滿足客戶需求。

▶ 熱衷於學習和建立技能，並且有能力在時間壓力下應付工作量。

　　提供住宿和經費，表現優良將有機會獲得高額獎金。必須能夠移居香港。

　　意者請將求職信和履歷寄至： Calista_Chen@anemailaddresslikethis.net

Task　1.7　▶參考答案

　　相信各位看得出來，黛西喜歡這份工作是因為她對國際稅法感興趣，這項職位能夠讓她學習擔任這個領域的稅務顧問，而且似乎和她的資歷程度相符。

　　透過目前的工作，黛西已經獲得企業客戶的稅務諮詢經驗，事業剛起步時她在陽光會計師事務所上班過，也得到諮詢小型企業客戶稅務的經驗。她在好不好塑膠公司工作時也有過小組管理的經驗。

　　現在我們來看一看黛西有意應徵的另一份工作。

Task 1.8

請閱讀下面這第四則求才廣告。以各位對黛西經驗和事業目標的了解，你覺得她為什麼會對這個職位感興趣？

● 求才廣告 IV

> ### KnowHow Inc.
> ### Financial Controller
>
> KnowHow Inc., a UK-based management consulting[1] company, is rapidly expanding in Asia. This position entails[2] the development and management of the Asian Finance Department, which includes a team of eight staff members located in Singapore.
>
> Job duties include:
>
> ▶ Production and submission of monthly management accounts
>
> ▶ Monthly forecasting and annual budgeting that includes financial strategic planning
>
> ▶ Production of group statutory[3] accounts and coordination of both internal and external auditing
>
> ▶ Review and development of system controls
>
> ▶ Tax planning and cost reduction
>
> We are looking for a qualified accountant with previous experience working in a fast-paced and growing company as an operationally focused financial controller. Special knowledge of UK culture, Asian culture, and Asian languages essential.
>
> Generous compensation package includes full health care, accommodation, company car, spending allowance, and holiday package.
>
> Please send a cover letter and CV to: Johnnie_Walker@anemailaddresslikethis.net

Word List

1 consult [kən`sʌlt] *v.* 擔任顧問
2 entail [ɪn`tel] *v.* 使負擔

3 statutory [`stætʃu͵torɪ] *adj.* 法定的

● 內容摘要

KnowHow Inc.
會計主管

　　本管理顧問公司位於倫敦，目前正快速往亞洲拓展事業。此職位將負責開發和經營位於新加坡的亞洲財務部門與旗下的團隊，團隊中有八名成員。

　　工作內容包括：

▸ 製作和提交月結管理帳戶表。

▸ 每月的估算預算和年度預算，包括財務策略規劃。

▸ 製作團體法定性財務報告，並協調內部與外部查帳審核。

▸ 審查和建立系統控制。

▸ 稅務規劃和節省成本。

　　我們徵求資格相符的會計師一名，過去曾經在步調快的成長中公司工作，並曾在該公司擔任過以營運為主的會計主管。掌握英國文化和亞洲文化及語言為必要條件。

　　薪酬待遇極佳，包括全套健保、住宿、公司汽車、優渥的生活費和休假福利。

　　意者請將求職信和 CV 寄至：Johnnie_Walker@anemailaddresslikethis.net

Task **1.8** ▸參考答案

　　這份工作會吸引黛西，是因為它可以讓她繼續加強客戶諮詢方面的經驗，同時還能建立國際觀的視野。

　　目前她在一家會計師事務所擔任稅務顧問，但過去在 BonK 上班時，就已獲取國內公司的財務管理經驗。該公司歷經合併之時，她擔任的是財務長，負責為新公司規畫和執行財務系統以及報表工具。所以這份工作可讓她在國際公司繼續發展這方面的專長。

　　此外，她在一家塑膠公司更獲得了小組管理的經驗，也有一些管理和改善系統、準備關鍵績效指標的經驗。

　　她的國際公認會計師公會會員資格是在英國考取的，也在英國住過一年，所以她覺得這項資歷不僅可吸引人資部的注意，同時也顯示出自己是對方心目中理想的面試人選。

　　現在我們來看一看黛西如何修改她的非目標式 CV，以凸顯出她符合這兩份求才廣告所開出的條件和資歷。

目標式 CV 3：職場老手篇

DAISY WANG	
Telephone: 0987 654 321	Email: Daisy.Wang@notmail.com
Date of Birth: 1970/05/06	Nationality: Taiwanese

PROFILE

A mature and committed[1] finance professional with excellent qualifications and wide experience. A Certified Public Accountant (ROC) and ACCA member with proven[2] track record in tax planning and cost saving. Practical expertise[3] in corporate financial management, including review and development of system controls and financial strategic planning. Special experience and interest in maximizing and improving financial reporting systems to assist in day-to-day decision making. Currently in final stage of part-time MBA focusing on international tax law.

POSITION

Financial Controller[4]

EDUCATION

2006 - present	MBA (part time) program, Nemme Hao University, Taiwan
2000	ACCA, Leicester University, UK
1994 - 1997	BA, Business Administration, Fei Chang Hao University, Taiwan.

WORK EXPERIENCE

2005 - present	Client service Manager, KPGM, Taiwan
	▸ Manage three major international corporate clients
	▸ Responsible for clients' ROC tax affairs

Word List

1 committed [kəˋmɪtɪd] *adj.* 致力的
2 proven [ˋpruvən] *adj.* 經過證明的
3 expertise [ˌɛkspɚˋtiz] *n.* 專門技術
4 controller [kənˋtrolɚ] *n.* 主管，管理人

2003 - 2005	**Assistant Manager, Finance Department, BonK Inc., Taiwan**

▸ Had sole responsibility for Taiwan branch financial affairs before merger

▸ Prepared management reports and KPI[5] for Taiwan office

▸ Participated in redesign of financial management systems

▸ Participated in long term strategic financial planning decisions before, during and after merger

▸ Oversaw audits for all subsidiaries

▸ Carried out annual tax audit

▸ Responsible for synchronization of tax affairs during merger

2001 - 2003	**Senior Auditor, Hao Bu Hao Plastics Corporation, Taiwan**

▸ Managed team of finance personnel

▸ Prepared EOY internal accounts and monthly KPIs

▸ Carried out annual tax audits

▸ Set up new financial reporting systems to facilitate[6] EOY accounts

▸ Successfully reduced taxation costs by 10% compared with previous post[7] holder for 2 years running

1997 - 2000	**Accountant Clerk, Sunshine Certified Public Accountants, Taiwan**

▸ Carried out annual tax audits for local small-to-medium sized companies

RELEVANT SKILLS

Fluent in Mandarin, Cantonese and English

Computer skills: Excel, Word, PowerPoint, FrontPage, Kerridge Systems, Reuters

Word List

5 KPI = Key Performance Indicators 7 post [post] *n.* 職位
關鍵績效指標

6 facilitate [fəˋsɪlə‚tet] *v.* 使便利

王黛西	
電話： 0987 654 321	電子郵件： Daisy.Wang@notmail.com
出生日期： 1970/05/06	國籍：台灣

個人簡介

　　成熟、忠誠的資深財務專業人員，條件優秀、經驗豐富。爲合格會計師（中華民國）和國際特許公認會計師會員，具財務規劃和節省成本的實務經驗。有實際的企業財務管理專長，包括審查和建立系統控制和財務策略規劃。在改善財務報表系統方面有特別經驗和興趣，可協助日常決策。目前兼職攻讀商管碩士學位已到最後一個階段，主修國際稅法。

應徵職位

財務主管

教育程度

2006 - 目前	台灣那麼好大學商管碩士（在職生）
2000	英國萊斯特大學國際公認特許會計師文憑
1994 - 1997	台灣非常好大學企業管理學士

工作經驗

2005 - 目前	台灣 KPGM 客戶服務經理
	▶ 負責三個主要國際企業客戶
	▶ 負責客戶在中華民國的稅務
2003 - 2005	台灣 BonK 財務部副理
	▶ 在公司合併之前，全權負責台灣分公司的財務
	▶ 爲台灣辦公室準備管理報告和關鍵績效指標
	▶ 參與財務管理系統的重新設計
	▶ 在公司合併之前、期間和之後均參與長期策略性財務規劃的決策
	▶ 監督所有子公司的查帳審核事務
	▶ 執行年度稅務查帳審核
	▶ 在公司合併過程中負責整合稅務

2001 - 2003	台灣好不好塑膠公司資深審計員
	▶ 負責領導一組財務人員工作團隊
	▶ 準備年終內部帳戶和月結關鍵績效指標
	▶ 執行年度稅務審計
	▶ 設立新的財務報表系統，輔助年終帳戶結算
	▶ 比起負責同一職位二年的前任員工，成功節省了一成的報稅成本
1997 - 2000	台灣陽光執業會計師事務所會計雇員
	▶ 為本地中小型企業做年度稅務查帳審核

相關技能

國語、廣東話、英文流利

電腦技能：Excel 、 Word 、 PowerPoint 、 FrontPage 、 Kerridge Systems 、 Reuters

目標式 CV 4：職場老手篇

DAISY WANG

Telephone: 0987 654 321	Email: Daisy.Wang@notmail.com
Date of Birth: 1970/05/06	Nationality: Taiwanese

PROFILE

A mature and meticulous[1] finance professional with excellent qualifications and wide experience. A Certified Public Accountant (ROC) and ACCA member with proven track record in increasing individuals' and corporations' tax savings in all kinds of taxation, from employer contributions to capital gains and stamp duty. Practical expertise in client management, financial systems development and international tax planning. Excellent at client relations management. Currently in final stage of part-time MBA focusing on international tax law.

POSITION

International Tax specialist

EDUCATION

2006 - present	MBA (part time) program, Nemme Hao University, Taiwan
2000	ACCA, Leicester University, UK
1994 - 1997	BA, Business Administration, Fei Chang Hao University, Taiwan.

WORK EXPERIENCE

2005 - present Client service Manager, KPGM, Taiwan

  ▸ Manage three major international corporate clients with businesses in three different tax environments

  ▸ Build and maintain relationship with new CFO and client finance team

  ▸ Trimmed tax costs by 5% across the board[2] in the first year

---

 Word List
1 meticulous [mə`tɪkjələs] *adj.* 小心謹慎的
2 across the board 全面地

▸ Reduced tax costs for one client by 25% by spotting and making use of a loophole[3] in regional tax laws

▸ Have overall responsibility for clients' ROC tax affairs

▸ Manage and develop a team of three

2003 - 2005 Assistant Manager, Finance Department, BonK Inc., Taiwan

▸ Oversaw audits for all subsidiaries

▸ Responsible for synchronization of tax affairs during merger

2001 - 2003 Senior Auditor, Hao Bu Hao Plastics Corporation, Taiwan

▸ Managed team of finance personnel

▸ Prepared EOY internal accounts and monthly KPIs

▸ Carried out annual tax audits

1997 - 2000 Accountant Clerk, Sunshine Certified Public Accountants, Taiwan

▸ Carried out annual tax audits for local small-to-medium sized companies

▸ Advised on tax issues and strategic financial planning for local and foreign entrepreneurs[4]

▸ Set up financial reporting systems for biggest client

▸ Built up and developed excellent relations with clients

▸ Brought in 5 new clients for the company, increasing revenues by 32%

RELEVANT SKILLS

Fluent in Mandarin, Cantonese and English

Computer skills: Excel, Word, PowerPoint, FrontPage, Kerridge Systems, Reuters

---

Word List

3 loophole [ˋlupˌhol] *n.* 漏洞

4 entrepreneur [ˌɑntrəprəˋnɝ] *n.* 企業家

王黛西	
電話： 0987 654 321	電子郵件： Daisy.Wang@notmail.com
出生日期： 1970/05/06	國籍：台灣

個人簡介

　　成熟、嚴謹的財務專業人員，條件優秀、經驗豐富。為合格會計師（中華民國）和國際特許公認會計師會員，從雇主供款到資本所得和印花稅，均有為個人和企業節省各項稅務成本的實務經驗。在客戶管理、財務系統建立和國際稅務規劃均有實際專長。客戶關係管理績效極佳。目前在職攻讀商管碩士學位已到最後一個階段，主修國際稅法。

應徵職位

國際稅務專員

教育程度

2006 - 目前	台灣那麼好大學商管碩士（在職生）
2000	英國萊斯特大學國際特許會計師文憑
1994 - 1997	台灣非常好大學企業管理學士

工作經驗

2005 - 目前	台灣 KPGM 客戶服務經理
	▸ 負責三個主要國際企業客戶，各有不同的稅務需求
	▸ 與新的首席財務長和客戶財務團隊建立和維持關係
	▸ 上任第一年即為董事會減少了 5% 的稅務成本
	▸ 發覺並善用當地稅法的一個漏洞，為一客戶節省了二成五的稅務成本
	▸ 全面負責客戶在中華民國的稅務
	▸ 管理和建立一組三人的工作團隊
2003 - 2005	台灣 BonK 財務部副理
	▸ 監督所有子公司的查帳審核事務
	▸ 在公司合併過程中負責整合稅務

2001 - 2003	台灣好不好塑膠公司資深審計員
	▸ 管理一組財務人員的工作團隊
	▸ 準備年終內部帳戶和月結關鍵績效指標
	▸ 執行年度稅務查帳審核
1997 - 2000	台灣陽光執業會計師事務所會計雇員
	▸ 為本地中小企業執行年度稅務查帳審核
	▸ 為本地和國外企業家提供稅務問題和策略性財務規劃的諮詢服務
	▸ 為最大客戶建立財務報表系統
	▸ 與客戶建立和發展絕佳關係
	▸ 為公司帶來五個新客戶，因而增加公司三成二的收入

相關技能

國語、廣東話、英文流利

電腦技能：Excel 、 Word 、 PowerPoint 、 FrontPage 、 Kerridge Systems 、
Reuters

Task 1.9

請閱讀前面兩份 CV ，找出所對應的求才廣告，並將 CV 號碼寫在下表右欄。

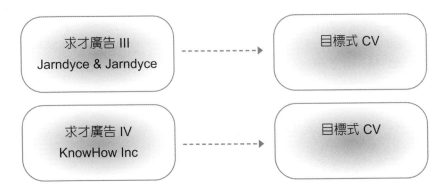

求才廣告 III
Jarndyce & Jarndyce
- - - - - ▸ 目標式 CV

求才廣告 IV
KnowHow Inc
- - - - - ▸ 目標式 CV

Task 1.9 ▶參考答案

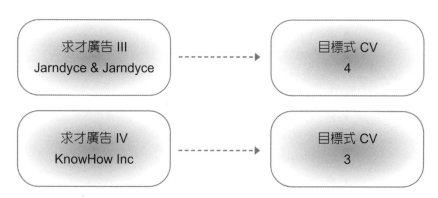

| 求才廣告 III Jarndyce & Jarndyce | - - - → | 目標式 CV 4 |
| 求才廣告 IV KnowHow Inc | - - - → | 目標式 CV 3 |

Task 1.10

請仔細研讀這兩份 CV。兩者之間有何相同和不同之處,又和原本的非目標式 CV 有何相同和不同之處?黛西如何配合求才廣告修改她的 CV,以凸顯她所具備的資歷符合雇主的要求?

Task 1.10 ▶參考答案

黛西和凱文一樣,配合求才廣告的條件修改了她 CV 中的相關資歷,以吸引雇主的目光。希望各位看得出來,為了讓所強調的資訊更加清楚而顯眼,黛西是如何補充說明 CV 中的部分資料,又是如何刪減其他部分的資料,以及黛西是如何分別修改了這兩份不同的個人簡介。除此之外,各位是否也注意到,這兩份 CV 中的文字依然力求簡潔,以詞彙為重?

現在我們就來分別更進一步研究黛西的這兩份 CV 吧。

目標式 CV3

▶ 在個人簡介中，黛西凸顯出她在 BonK 和好不好塑膠公司的工作經驗，並將重點放在每日的財務管理和長期的策略規畫方面。她希望藉由這方面的經驗吸引雇主的注意。

▶ 在 CV 的主體中，黛西選擇將兩份工作經歷加以補充說明，也就是在 BonK 和塑膠公司擔任會計暨財務經理的時候。在 BonK 的職務方面，她將焦點放在公司合併之前、期間和之後她所做的貢獻。她特別凸顯她在重新設計和改善財務記錄保存系統方面的經驗，以表現出她既能處理每日細節，也能做長期策略計畫的才幹，因為她相信這兩種才能是她最特別的強項，而且招聘人員要找到兼具兩種才能的人才並不容易。

▶ 她還詳述了她在塑膠公司的工作內容，具體舉出她對該公司的貢獻。

目標式 CV4

▶ 在個人簡介中，黛西凸顯她在公共會計事務所擔任外部顧問的經驗，以及客戶關係的專長和對客戶所做的貢獻。

▶ 在 CV 的主體部分，她詳述了擔任外部顧問會計師時的工作內容，並刪減了當內控會計暨財務經理的敘述，因為她相信對方不會太重視這些資歷。

▶ 描述 KPGM 的資歷時，黛西選擇凸顯她曾為客戶減少成本的成果，並以數字舉證。如果招聘人員在面試時向她詢問數據的話，她有記錄以供佐證。在同一段敘述當中，她更特別指出她在建立客戶關係的長才，並提到她曾擔任小組經理的經驗。她希望招聘人員對這類經驗感興趣。

▶ 陽光會計師事務所是她服務的第一家公司，距今已有一段時日，不過在敘述當中，黛西仍特別強調她當時的成就，表示不論聘僱公司所處的產業為何，她都能為公司創造價值。她現今的經驗都與企業客戶的諮詢顧問有關，但求才廣告中明白指出新職位會需要提供高收入的個人客戶稅務方面的諮詢，因此黛西提到她曾為在台設立公司的外商諮詢的經驗。她希望這些資歷足以引起招聘人員的興趣，想在面試時進一步了解她這方面的經驗。

求職達人基本功：個人簡介

　　我們已經研究過了一些 CV，各位對如何針對特定求才廣告修改 CV，以提高爭取面試的機會也已有一些概念，現在我們來進一步學習 CV 會用到的詞彙吧。在此我們將側重個人簡介的撰寫方式，下一單元則將介紹一些可用於 CV 和求職信的動詞。

Task 1.11

　　請研讀以下用於個人簡介中的第一個句子，各位看得出這些句子在結構上有何相似之處嗎？

▶ A reliable and dedicated financial professional with more than twelve years experience in a broad range of segments.

▶ A promising and entrepreneurial business administration major with a strong interest in logistics and sales.

▶ A responsible and trustworthy financial professional with proven experience of achieving cost savings.

▶ An enthusiastic and hard working business administration major with a strong interest in marketing and event management.

▶ An enterprising and proactive business administration major with experience in retail and wholesale sales.

▶ A mature and meticulous finance professional with excellent qualifications and wide experience.

Task 1.11 ▶參考答案

　　在現實世界中，其實這些句子完全算不上是句子，因為裡面沒有動詞片語。這些句子不過是一長串的 word partnerships 罷了。請做下面的練習來了解這種寫法。

Task 1.12

請用方框中的語詞填空，完成下列各個句子。請見第一句的示範。

1
(1) a broad range of segments
(2) more than 12 years experience
(3) reliable and dedicated

A ____*(3)*____ financial professional with _____ in _____ .

2
(1) a strong interest
(2) enthusiastic and hard working
(3) marketing and event management

An _____ business administration major with _____ in _____ .

3
(1) retail and wholesale sales
(2) business administration major
(3) enterprising

An _____ and proactive _____ with experience in _____ .

4
(1) excellent qualifications
(2) finance professional
(3) wide experience

A mature and meticulous _____ with _____ and _____ .

Task 1.12 ▶參考答案

請利用 Task 1.11 的句子與自己所填的答案做比較。

Task 1.13

現在請比照剛剛研究過的句子來造句描述自己。

現在就讓我們來學習一些如何描述自己的詞彙吧。

Task 1.14

請看以下這些用來描述人格特質的形容詞，哪些適合用來描述你自己？哪些適合用在你所處的領域？

03

求職必備語庫 1.1

active	活躍的	keen	熱衷的
caring	有愛心的	kind	親切的
committed	堅定的	knowledgeable	博學的
compassionate	有同情心的	mature	成熟的
considerate	周到的	productive	多產的
creative	有創意的	qualified	合格的
dedicated	專注的	reliable	可信賴的
devoted	專心致志的	resourceful	資源豐富的
dynamic	有活力的	responsible	負責任的
energetic	精力旺盛的	skilled	有技能的
enthusiastic	熱心的	stable	穩定的
experienced	經驗豐富的	steady	沉著的
inventive	善於創造的	trustworthy	可信的
dependable	可靠的		

Task **1.14** ▶參考答案

　　請小心使用這些形容詞，其中有些可能不適合你所處的行業。例如，如果你是會計師，最好不要選用 caring 和 creative 這類情感性字眼；如果你在醫療界工作，則最好不要選用 inventive 和 productive 這類績效導向的字詞。

Task **1.15**

　　下面是一些形容領域、行業和公司部門的形容詞。各位是在哪個領域工作呢？

求職必備語庫 1.2

accounting	computing	legal	public sector
advertising	financial	manufacturing	research
agricultural	HR	marketing	sales
banking	insurance	medical	telemarketing
business	IT	pharmaceutical	tourism

Task **1.16**

　　請看下列這些可以用於個人簡介的 chunks。並且回到本單元的前面部分，從各位先前已研讀過的 CV 個人簡介中，找出下表中的 chunks 並畫上底線。此外，也請注意這些 chunks 在個人簡介中的用法。

求職必備語庫 1.3

... (special) responsibility for ...	... all aspects of ...
... in a broad range of areas ...	... experience of ...
... with (special) expertise in ...	... as well as ...
... experience includes ...	... with a commitment to ...
... including ...	... (special) emphasis on ...
... with almost ...	... reporting to ...
... current interest in ...	... much of it ...
... current work in ...	... with more than ...
... many aspects of ...	... many of them ...

Task 1.17

請利用前面必備語庫 1.3 中的 chunks 填空,完成下列這份個人簡介。

An experienced and committed accounting professional (1)_____ 12 years experience, (2)_____ as a tax consultant. (3)_____ (4)_____ taxation, (5)_____ employer contributions, VAT and other sales taxes, stamp duty and capital gains tax. (6)_____ international tax regulations.

Task 1.17 ▶參考答案

以下提供建議答案:

(1) with more than/
   with almost
(2) much of it/
   many of them
(3) With (special) expertise in/
   With (special) emphasis on/
   Experience includes
(4) many aspects of/
   all aspects of
(5) including/
   as well as
(6) Current interest in/
   Current work in

Task 1.18

現在就請各位開始為非目標式 CV 撰寫個人簡介吧。

求職達人基本功：詞彙應用（一）

　　在本單元結束之前，在此要介紹如何將求才廣告中的詞彙應用在個人簡介中，這也算是撰寫目標式 CV 的一種方法。

Task　1.19

　　請比較求才廣告 I 和 II（Expressways Resin 和 Clerks）的詞彙表，然後與目標式 CV 1 和 2 的個人簡介做比較。有哪些詞彙既出現在求才廣告中，又出現在 CV 中？完成下表的勾選。請注意這些詞彙的用法，好讓 CV 更貼近目標式。

	求才廣告 I	目標式 CV 2
Sales	✓	✓
Logistics		
Technical		
Excited by opportunities		
Career development		
Motivated by the challenge		
Learning new skills		
Inventory management		
	求才廣告 II	目標式 CV 1
Creative input		
Managing customer inquiries		
Marketing event management		
Selling		
Budget management		

Task 1.19 ▶參考答案

請以下表與自己勾選的答案做比較。如果沒有找出下表中的所有詞彙，請再找一次！

	求才廣告 I	目標式 CV 2
Sales	✓	✓
Logistics	✓	✓
Technical	✓	✓
Excited by opportunities	✓	-
Career development	✓	-
Motivated by the challenge	✓	-
Learning new skills	✓	-
Inventory management	✓	✓
	求才廣告 II	目標式 CV 1
Creative input	✓	-
Managing customer inquiries	✓	✓
Marketing event management	✓	-
Selling	✓	-
Budget management	✓	✓

Task **1.20**

　　請比較求才廣告 III 和 IV（Jarndyce & Jarndyce 和 KnowHow Inc.）的詞彙表，
然後與目標式 CV 3 和 4 中的個人簡介做比較。有哪些詞彙既出現在求才廣告中，又
出現在 CV 中？完成下表的勾選。請注意詞彙的用法，好讓 CV 更貼近目標式。

	求才廣告 III	目標式 CV 4
International tax planning	✓	✓
Individuals and corporations		
Employer contributions		
Capital gains		
Stamp duty		
Tax solutions		
Excellent client relations		
Keen to learn and develop new technical skills		
	求才廣告 IV	目標式 CV 3
Review and development of system controls		
Financial strategic planning		
Tax planning		
Cost reduction		
External auditing		
Internal auditing		

Task 1.20 ▶ 參考答案

請以下表與自己勾選的答案做比較。如果沒有找出下表中的所有詞彙，請再找一次！

	求才廣告 III	目標式 CV 4
International tax planning	✓	✓
Individuals and corporations	✓	✓
Employer contributions	✓	✓
Capital gains	✓	✓
Stamp duty	✓	✓
Tax solutions	✓	-
Excellent client relations	✓	✓
Keen to learn and develop new technical skills	✓	-
	求才廣告 IV	目標式 CV 3
Review and development of system controls	✓	✓
Financial strategic planning	✓	✓
Tax planning	✓	✓
Cost reduction	✓	✓
External auditing	✓	-
Internal auditing	✓	-

Task 1.21

現在就請拿出自己的個人簡介，專為某個有意應徵的求才廣告進行改寫吧。

好啦，本單元的學習就到此結束。希望各位已經學會針對特定工作條件撰寫目標式 CV。在繼續往下一單元學習之前，請回到本單元前面的學習目標清單，確認是否每一項目標都達成。如果還有不甚明白之處，可回去重新研讀一次，直到確實理解爲止。

Unit ②

求職信
The Cover Letter

 # 引言與學習目標

各位還記得我們在上一單元看到的幾份求才廣告嗎？在這個單元中，我們要學習的便是如何針對那些求才廣告撰寫目標式求職信，也會學習如何撰寫非目標式的求職信。

在本單元學習結束之前，各位應該達成的學習目標如下：

❏ 得到一些通用的訣竅，懂得如何寫出專業的求職信。
❏ 知道在求職信中應該寫些什麼內容，以及如何發展內容架構。
❏ 理解目標式和非目標式求職信之間的差異，以及撰寫目標式求職信時的考量。
❏ 學會在求職信中重複運用求才廣告中的語彙，讓求職信更目標化。
❏ 學會一些可用於求職信中不同段落的 set-phrases。
❏ 學到一些可用來撰寫求職信和 CV 的動詞。
❏ 學會變換句子結構，為求留給對方英文能力優異的良好印象。
❏ 做過求職信的寫作練習。

非目標式求職信

　　非目標式求職信事實上比目標式的更難撰寫，因為若各位的腦海中沒有設定展信者或特別希望應徵的工作，撰寫求職信時往往不知從何下筆，應該提供哪些資訊才好。

　　在撰寫非目標式求職信時，最好是選擇一、二個最高的工作成就當做重點加以說明。就讓我們先來看一看凱文和黛西的作法吧。

Task　2.1

　　請看這兩份非目標式求職信，並與前一個單元的非目標式 CV 進行比較。各位看得出有哪些相同和不同之處嗎？

非目標式求職信：職場新手篇

P.O.Box 1234567 Taipei 106, Taiwan
Telephone: 0912 345 678
Email: Kevin11@notmail.com

Month, Day, Year

Company Name
Company Address

Dear Sir/Madam,

I am writing in the hope that you have a vacancy for an ambitious and promising business administration graduate in your sales or marketing department.

You will see from my attached CV that I have experience and interest in the sales, logistics, and marketing fields. I already have some experience with these fields from my vacation jobs.

I have recently worked as a marketing assistant for Taipei 101 as a member of a team of eight responsible for planning and implementing the Taipei 101 anniversary event. This event comprised[1] a booth on the main floor of the mall containing an exhibition about the building, and an inquiry desk for office and retail space rental. I participated in all aspects of the project, from planning to procurement,[2] to setting up and dealing with customer and walk-through[3] inquiries. I took care of the design and production of the DM in accordance with[4] the brief[5] from the marketing department, and led a small group responsible for distribution of the DM.

Word List

1. comprise [kəmˋpraɪz] v. 包含
2. procurement [prəˋkjuəmənt] n. 採購
3. walk-through adj. 門市的；現場的
4. in accordance with 一致；依照
5. brief [brif] n. 簡報；指示

In the summer of 2006 I worked as a temporary sales clerk for Campho Ltd., a photographic equipment manufacturer and exporter.[6] While at Campho my duties included selling to overseas buyers, demonstrating the equipment and matching new products with existing customers. Among my achievements for Campho were bringing in bulk orders worth NT$6 and NT$9.5 million respectively from two new customers through my contacts as treasurer of my university Photographers Association. I was also responsible for maintaining after sales service, for which I set up and systematized[7] a customer inquiry database to assist in providing a more targeted after-sales service.

In addition to this experience of sales and event management, I am the treasurer of the university Photographers Association. My responsibilities here include the collection of membership dues, budgeting for events and activities, and balancing the club accounts. I have held this position for two years, during which time club revenues have increased by 34 percent.

I am enthusiastic, capable of taking the initiative, and eager to learn. I believe I would be a suitable addition[8] to your team. I would be interested in talking with you further about what opportunities you have.

I look forward to hearing from you.

Yours faithfully,

Kevin Gao

Kevin Gao

Word List

6. exporter [ɪksˋportə] *n.* 出口商
7. systematize [ˋsɪstəməˏtaɪz] *v.* 系統化
8. addition [əˋdɪʃən] *n.* 新成員

106 台北郵政信箱 1234567

電話： 0912 345 678

電子信箱：Kevin11@notmail.com

本日日期

公司名稱
公司地址

敬啓者：

　　本人在校主修企業管理學，企圖心強、前途有爲，特來信應徵貴公司業務部或行銷部之職，期貴公司予以考慮僱用。

　　從所附的履歷表可得知本人在業務、物流和行銷領域均有經驗並有高度興趣，在過去放假期間已在這些領域得到一些工作經驗。

　　本人近期曾在台北 101 擔任過行銷助理，爲八人小組的一員，負責規畫和執行台北 101 的週年慶活動。此活動在購物中心的主要樓層皆設有攤位，展示有關大樓的資訊，另設有一諮詢台，專門回答辦公室和零售商店等出租問題。舉凡計畫、採購、搭建到客戶服務以及現場回答問題，本人全程參與此計畫的所有工作項目，亦根據行銷部的簡報設計並製作 DM，此外，還帶領一個小團隊負責分發 DM。

　　在 2006 年夏天，本人曾在 Campho 擔任臨時售貨員。Campho 爲一家攝影設備製造商和出口商。在 Campho 任職期間，本人職責包括對國外買家銷售產品，以及爲現有客戶示範操作和推薦適合的新產品。對 Campho 的貢獻包括透過在大學攝影社當財務股長的人脈，爲公司帶來兩個新客戶，客戶所下的大宗訂單各爲公司帶來價值新台幣 600 和 950 萬元的收入。此外，本人亦負責維持產品的售後服務，為此特別建立了客戶詢問資料庫，並將之系統化以提供更具目標化的售後服務。

　　除了以上業務和活動管理的經驗之外，本人曾擔任大學攝影社的財務股長，在社團中的職責包括收取會費、編列節目和活動預算，以及為社團的收支記帳。本人擔任此職位達二年之久，期間並將社團收入提高三成四之多。

　　本人個性熱心、主動積極而且好學不倦，深具自信將會是貴公司團隊的合適人選。期與貴公司談論可能的工作機會。

　　靜候回音

高凱文　敬上

非目標式求職信：職場老手篇

P.O.Box 765432 Taipei 106, Taiwan
Telephone: 0987 654 321
Email: Daisy.Wang@notmail.com

Month, Day, Year

Company Name
Company Address

Dear Sir/Madam,

I am writing in the hope that you have a vacant position for a qualified and mature tax specialist and finance manager in your company.

You will see from my attached CV that I am a CPA and ACCA member with proven experience in providing corporations and individuals with tax solutions. I have excellent customer relations skills, and experience in utilizing[1] international tax environments to make tax cost savings for my clients. I am also interested in renewing and developing my experience of in-company financial management, especially in a rapid growth situation, as I already have some experience with this.

For the last two years I have been working as a client service manager and tax consultant with KPGM. My present position mainly involves managing ROC tax affairs in all areas of taxation for three international corporate clients with operations in Taiwan, two of whom are in the IT sector, and one in the pharmaceutical[2] sector. I have been able to achieve average tax savings of 5 percent

Word List

1. utilize [ˈjutḷˌaɪz] v. 派上用場
2. pharmaceutical [ˌfɑrməˈsjutɪkḷ] adj. 製藥的

96

for all my clients within one year. In addition, I increased tax savings by 25 percent for one client in particular by utilizing loopholes in regional offshore tax regulations. I have been able to develop and maintain excellent relations with the new CFO[3] of one of my clients. This has resulted in increased business for my company.

From 2003 to 2005 I held the position of Assistant Manager in the Finance Department for BonK. During this time, BonK merged with System Integrated Silica Controls Ltd. Before the merger I focused on the day-to-day operations of the finance department, including supervising[4] a team of fifteen. I collected data on KPI and compiled[5] management reports, including monthly forecasting and preparing recommendations for annual budgets.

I am scrupulous[6], hard working, and proactive in looking for tax cost savings. I am currently in the final stages of my MBA, writing up my thesis on international tax law, focusing on the Asia-Pacific Region. I believe I would be a suitable addition to your team. I would be interested in talking with you further about what opportunities you have.

I look forward to hearing from you.

Yours faithfully,

Daisy Wang
Daisy Wang

Word List

3. CFO = chief financial officer 財務長
4. supervise [ˈsupɚˌvaɪz] *v.* 監督
5. compile [kəmˈpaɪl] *v.* 收集編撰
6. scrupulous [ˈskrupjələs] *adj.* 謹慎的

106 台北郵政信箱 765432
電話： 0987 654 321
電子信箱：Daisy.Wang@notmail.com

本日日期

公司名稱
公司地址

敬啟者：

　　本人資歷優異、歷練成熟，特來信應徵貴公司稅務專員與財務經理之職，盼貴公司予以考慮僱用。

　　從所附的履歷表可得知本人為執業會計師與國際特許公認會計師會員，具有為企業和個人提供報稅服務的實際經驗。客戶關係技巧極佳，曾利用國際稅制為客戶節省稅務成本，也非常有興趣重拾並發展在公司內部財務管理方面的經驗，尤其是在成長快速的公司環境中，況且本人已具有此方面相當豐富的經驗。

　　在過去兩年當中，本人一直在 KPGM 擔任客服經理與稅務顧問。目前的職務主要是負責管理三個國際企業客戶在中華民國各個方面的稅務，其中有兩個客戶是在資訊科技業，另一個是在藥劑業。本人曾在一年內為所有客戶成功節省了5% 的稅。此外亦曾利用地區性海外稅制的漏洞，特為一個客戶額外節省了二成五的稅。本人與其中一個客戶新上任的首席財務長建立並維持極好的關係，因而為公司帶來更高的收入。

　　自 2003 至 2005 年，本人在 BonK 擔任財務部副理一職，期間 BonK 與 System Integrated Silica Controls 合併。在合併之前，本人主要負責財務部的日常運作，包括監督一個 15 人小組。本人亦搜集關於關鍵績效指標的資料和彙整管理報告，其中包括每月預測報告和準備提報有關編列年度預算的建議。

　　本人謹慎細心、工作勤奮，並積極尋找節稅方案。目前正在攻讀商管碩士學位的最後階段，撰寫的論文以國際稅法為題，並以亞太地區為研究重點。本人自信會是貴公司團隊的適當人選，期與貴公司進一步討論可能的工作機會。

　　靜候回音

王黛西　敬上

Task 2.1 ▶參考答案

　　讓我們來看一下這兩份求職信的相同和不同之處。

相同處

▶ 兩封求職信都只有一頁長。

▶ 兩封求職信都將本人的聯絡資料放在頁面的左上方，收件公司的地址也在頁面的左方，並低於本人的地址，同時日期也是寫在左方，亦即介於收件和寄件地址之間，而且兩封信的上款都用 Dear Sir/Madam，至於下款也以 Yours faithfully 結尾。在不是特定收信對象的情況之下，下款敬語便應該用 Yours faithfully。

▶ 兩封求職信都開宗明義地表明了來信意圖。第二段則請收信者展讀所附的履歷表，並自我介紹專長和資歷。有關這一段的用語將於本單元的後面再行介紹。

▶ 接下來有兩個段落是專門敘述自己達成的某項業績。

▶ 最後一段則是描述求職者的個人特質，同時表示希望得到公司的回音。這一段的用語容後介紹。

▶ 這兩封求職信的文字都簡單易讀，句子結構也非常好。這種句子的寫法將在後面介紹。

不同處

▸ 這兩者最大的不同在於信的內容。

▸ 凱文選擇以台北 101 的行銷經驗當作說明重點。他簡短描述了在台北 101 的工作內容，藉此表現他既能主動辦事，在團隊中也有合作精神。台北 101 是他目前服務過的公司中最知名的一家，這也是他選擇在求職信中特別說明這份工作的原因。撰寫求職信時，最好選擇曾經服務過規模最大、知名度最高的公司，將當時的工作內容當作重點補充說明。

▸ 凱文也選擇凸顯在 Campho 的售貨和物流經驗，並舉出一些實例具體證明他對該公司的貢獻。所以撰寫這部分時，最好盡量提供一些類似的實例，讓未來的雇主知道你會是公司的寶貴資源。

▸ 凱文也選擇凸顯在攝影社當財務股長時的業績，顯示他有處理財務的經驗。

▸ 黛西決定強調她在目前工作擔任外部稅務顧問的經驗，以及在上一間公司 BonK 上班時的內部經驗，因為這兩份工作最能代表她資歷中的兩大領域。稍後在本單元中，將介紹各位用哪些動詞時態來描述目前和過去的工作。

▸ 描述在 KPGM 任職時期的職務時，黛西把焦點放在她和客戶的關係上，同時以實例證明她對客戶所做的貢獻。

▸ 在說明 BonK 的職務那一段中，黛西把重點放在她於公司合併過程中獲得的經驗和所扮演的角色，以凸顯自己的組織和策略能力。

▸ 凱文和黛西會選擇這些範例作為解說重點，是因為他們想要呈現的是各種不同的長處和經驗，而不是集中說明某一特定的長處或經驗。由於這封非目標式求職信是用來搭配非目標式 CV 的，所以他們會希望盡量擴大選擇範圍。

希望各位已經都了解凱文和黛西在撰寫求職信時的各項考量了。

Task 2.2

　　請撰寫並研讀自己的非目標式求職信。依據本節所學到的新知，各位覺得應如何修改自己的求職信？

　　現在請繼續往下研究目標式求職信，並學習發展求職信的內容架構。

目標式求職信

我們就先從凱文的目標式求職信開始學起吧。

Task　2.3

　　請閱讀以下凱文的兩封目標式求職信，找出上一單元中所對應的求才廣告，並完成下表格。

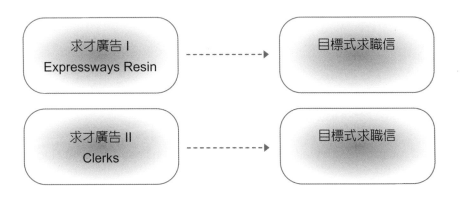

目標式求職信 1：職場新手篇

P.O.Box 1234567 Taipei 106, Taiwan
Telephone: 0912 345 678
Email: Kevin11@notmail.com

Month Day, Year

Mr. Bill Sikes
HR Manager
Clerks
12 Guanqian Rd., 11th Floor Taipei 106, Taiwan

Dear Mr. Sikes,

I am writing in connection with the advert for a Trade Fair Event Trainee Manager with Clerks listed on www.104.com.tw.

You will see from my attached CV that I am a business major at Hao Li Hai University.

I am currently in the final stages of my dissertation[1] on marketing in China, and will be graduating this June. I am especially interested in the creative and practical aspects of marketing. I already have some experience with marketing event management, sales, dealing with customer inquiries, and budget management from my vacation jobs.

I have recently worked as an event management assistant for Taipei 101 as a member of a team of eight responsible for planning and implementing the Taipei 101 anniversary event. This event comprised a booth on the main floor of the mall containing an exhibition about the building, and an inquiry desk for office and retail space rental. I participated in all aspects of the project, from

Word List 1. dissertation [ˌdɪsəˈteʃən] *n.* 學術論文

planning to procurement, to setting up and managing customer and walk-through inquiries. I took care of the design and production of the DM, including creative input, in accordance with the brief from the marketing department, and led a small group responsible for distribution of the DM.

In the summer of 2006 I worked as a sales clerk for Campho, a photo-graphic equipment manufacturer and exporter. My duties included dealing with customer inquiries, and processing bulk orders from inquiry to shipping. Among my achievements for Campho were bringing in orders worth NT$6 and NT$9.5 million respectively from two new customers through my contacts as treasurer of my university Photographers Association.

I have experience with sales and customer inquires from my part time vacation jobs in my local 7-Eleven, where I also managed a team of three sales clerks. I also worked as a desk clerk at Hai Hao La Buxiban, where I dealt with customer inquiries on the phone, and achieved the highest sales target of the summer.

In addition to this experience with sales and event management, I am the treasurer of the university Photographers Association. My responsibilities here include the collection of membership dues, budgeting for events and activities, and balancing the club accounts. I have held this position for two years, during which time club revenues have increased by 34 percent.

I am enthusiastic, capable of taking initiative, and eager to learn. I believe I am suitably qualified and experienced for the job advertised. I would be inter-ested in talking with you further about what opportunities you have.

I look forward to hearing from you.

Yours sincerely,

Kevin Gao

Kevin Gao

106 台北郵政信箱 1234567

電話： 0912 345 678

電子信箱：Kevin11@notmail.com

本日日期

比爾・賽克思先生

人資部經理

Clerks

台北市館前路 12 號 11 樓

敬愛的賽克思先生：

　　本人自 <u>www.104.com.tw</u> 獲悉貴公司徵求商展活動培訓經理一名，特來信應徵。

　　從所附的履歷表可得知本人爲好厲害大學的商學院學生。

　　目前本人正在撰寫論文的最後階段，論文以在大中華行銷爲題，將於今年六月畢業。本人對行銷的創意與實務方面尤感興趣，在行銷活動管理已有些許經驗，曾在放假打工時負責銷售及處理客戶詢問與預算管理等事務。

　　近期內本人曾在台北 101 擔任過活動管理助理，爲八人小組的一員，負責規畫和執行台北 101 的週年慶活動。此活動包括在購物中心的主要樓層皆設有攤位，展示大樓的相關資訊，另設有一諮詢台，專門回答辦公室與零售店出租資訊。舉凡計畫、採購、搭建到客戶服務以及現場回答問題，本人全程參與了此計畫的所有工作項目，亦根據行銷部的簡報設計並製作 DM，包括貢獻創意，此外，並帶領一個小團隊分發 DM。

　　在 2006 年夏天，本人曾在 Campho 擔任售貨員一職，Campho 爲一家攝影設備製造商暨出口商。本人職務包括處理客戶的詢問，並從詢問到寄運一手包辦大宗訂單。本人在 Campho 的成就包括透過在大學攝影社擔任財務股長的人脈，為公司帶來兩個新客戶，客戶所下的訂單各為公司帶來價值新台幣 600 和 950 萬元的收入。

　　本人在放假期間曾在住家附近的 7-Eleven 兼差，具有售貨和客戶服務經驗，亦曾負責帶領一個三人售貨員小組。此外也曾在還好拉補習班擔任辦事員一職，處理客戶的來電詢問，並達到暑期最高業績目標。

　　除了售貨和活動管理的經驗之外，本人亦曾擔任大學攝影社的財務股長，在社團中的職責包括收取會費，編列節目和活動預算以及為社團的收支記帳。本人擔任此職位達二年之久，期間並將社團收入提高三成四。

　　本人個性熱心、主動並且好學不倦，自信定能符合貴公司求才廣告所列之條件和必備經驗。期與貴公司談論可能的工作機會。

　　靜候回音

高凱文　　敬上

目標式求職信 2：職場新手篇

P.O.Box 1234567 Taipei 106, Taiwan
Telephone:0912 345 678
Email: Kevin11@notmail.com

Month Day, Year

Ms. Nancy Drew
Senior Administrative Assistant
Expressways Resin
12 Guanqian Rd., 11th Floor Taipei 106, Taiwan

Dear Ms. Drew,

　　I am writing in connection with the advert for sales and logistics personnel in the *Taipei Times* 6 March 2007.

　　You will see from my attached CV that I am a business major at Hao Li Hai University.

　　I am currently in the final stages of my dissertation on marketing in China, which includes a chapter on the importance of logistics and distribution. I will graduate this June. I am excited by the opportunities for career development in this field, and I already have some experience with technical sales and marketing from my vacation jobs.

　　In the summer of 2006 I worked as a temporary sales clerk for Campho Ltd., a photographic equipment manufacturer and exporter. While at Campho my duties included selling to overseas buyers, demonstrating the equipment, and matching new products with existing customers. Among my achievements for Campho were bringing in bulk orders worth NT$6 and NT$9.5 million respectively from two new customers through my contacts as treasurer of my university Photographers Association. I was also responsible for maintaining after sales service, for which I set up and systematized a customer inquiry database to assist in providing a more targeted after-sales service.

I also worked as a stock[1] control clerk for Costco during the busy Christmas and Chinese New Year season of 2006. My job there was to assist in the management of green goods supply. This is particularly challenging, as these goods are perishable[2] and cannot be stored[3] for long. Prompt delivery of new stock is essential. I established good relations with new and existing suppliers and was able to keep the store continuously well stocked in spite of the unpredictable peaks and troughs[4] in demand.

In 2005 I worked as a sales clerk in my local 7-Eleven store, where I learned the basics of inventory management. While there I reorganized the storeroom and created more space for storage and thus reduced the need for frequent deliveries. I identified some problems with the in-store inventory controls and upgraded them. I was given the responsibility of training other sales clerks in the new system. I also worked as a telemarketer[5] for Hai Hao La Buxiban in the summer of 2004, and achieved the highest sales targets of the summer.

I am enthusiastic, capable of taking initiative, motivated by challenges, and eager to learn new skills. I believe I am suitably qualified and experienced for the job advertised. I would be interested in talking with you further about what opportunities you have.

I look forward to hearing from you.

Sincerely yours,

Kevin Gao
Kevin Gao

Word List

1. stock [stɑk] *n.* 庫存
2. perishable [ˈpɛrɪʃəbl] *a.* 易腐的
3. store [stor] *v.* 儲存
4. trough [trɔf] *n.* 低谷
5. telemarketer [ˈtɛləˌmɑrkɪtə] *n.* 電話行銷員

106 台北郵政信箱 1234567

電話： 0912 345 678

電子郵件： Kevin@hotmail.com

本日日期

南希・朱小姐

資深行政助理

Expressways Resin

台北市館前路 12 號 11 樓

敬愛的朱女士：

　　本人於 2007 年 3 月 6 日自《台北時報》獲悉貴公司徵求業務和物流員工一名，特來信應徵。

　　從所附的履歷表可得知本人為好厲害大學的商學院學生。

　　目前本人正在撰寫論文的最後階段，論文以在大中華行銷為題，且其中有一章是關於物流和配銷的重要性，將於今年六月畢業。本人非常期待能有機會在此領域發展生涯，故在過去放假打工時已在技術性業務和行銷方面有過一些經驗。

　　在 2006 年夏，本人曾在 Campho 擔任臨時售貨員。 Campho 為一家攝影設備製造商暨出口商。在 Campho 任職期間，本人職責包括對國外買家銷售產品，以及為現有客戶示範操作和推薦適合的新產品。在 Campho 的成就之一為透過在大學攝影社擔任財務股長的人脈，為公司帶來兩個新客戶，客戶所下的大宗訂單各為公司帶來價值新台幣 600 和 950 萬元的收入。此外，本人亦負責維持產品的售後服務，為此特別建立了客戶詢問資料庫，並將之系統化以提供更具目標化的售後服務。

本人亦曾在繁忙的聖誕節和 2005 年春節期間在好市多擔任庫存控制員，職責為協助綠色生鮮產品的供給管理。此職務甚具挑戰性，因為綠色生鮮產品容易毀損，不能長久儲存，新貨的快速寄運非常重要。本人與新舊供應商建立了良好關係，得以在不穩定的高峰期和低谷期持續維持適當的庫存水準。

在 2005 年，本人在社區中的 7-Eleven 打工，因而學到了存貨管理的基本須知。此外，在工作期間並幫商店重整儲藏空間，以挪出更多空間儲藏貨物，故可降低訂貨頻率。本人甚至發現店內存貨控制上的一些問題並將系統升級。後來被指派訓練其他售貨員使用新系統。本人也曾於 2004 年在還好拉補習班從事電話行銷員一職，並達到暑期最高業績目標。

本人個性熱心、主動積極、不畏挑戰且學習新技能的意願高，自信定能符合貴公司求才廣告所列之條件和必備經驗。期與貴公司談論可能的工作機會。

靜候回音

高凱文　敬上

Task **2.3** ▶參考答案

請利用下表核對答案。

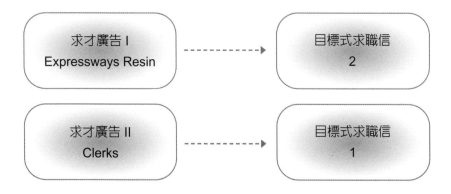

現在我們來看一看黛西的目標式求職信。

Task 2.4

請閱讀以下黛西的兩封目標式求職信，找出上一單元中所對應的求才廣告，並完成下表格。

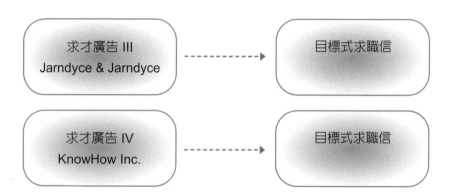

目標式求職信 3：職場老手篇

P.O.Box 765432 Taipei 106, Taiwan
Telephone: 0987 654 321
Email: Daisy.Wang@notmail.com

Month Day, Year

Mr. Johnnie Walker
Accounting Manager
KnowHow Inc.
12 Guanqian Rd., 11th Floor
Taipei 106, Taiwan

Dear Mr. Walker,

I am writing in connection with the advert for financial controller in the *Financial Times* 6 March 2007.

You will see from my attached CV that I am a CPA and ACCA member with proven experience in the review and development of financial controls, and in achieving tax cost reduction through careful tax planning.

I am currently working as a client service manager and tax consultant with KPGM, where I have been for two years. My job includes managing ROC tax affairs for three international corporate clients with operations in Taiwan, two of whom are in the IT sector, and one in the pharmaceutical sector. I am interested in renewing and developing my experience of in-house financial management, especially in a rapid growth situation, and I already have some experience with this.

From 2003 to 2005 I held the position of Assistant Manager in the Finance Department at BonK. During this time, BonK merged with System Integrated Silica Controls Ltd. Before the merger I focused on the day-to-day operations of the finance department, including supervising a team of fifteen. I collected data on KPI and compiled management reports, including monthly forecasting and preparing recommendations for annual budgets. In addition, I oversaw[1] all external auditing. During the lead-up[2] to the merger I facilitated the redesign of financial system controls and participated in long-term financial strategic planning for the newly merged company. In addition, I also coordinated with the SISC financial department and oversaw the synchronization of tax affairs of the two companies in order to expedite[3] the first internal audit of the newly merged company.

From 2001 to 2003 I was Senior Auditor at Hao Bu Hao Plastics Corporation, where I directed a team of twelve finance personnel. As well as executing my internal and external auditing responsibilities, I also overhauled[4] the company financial systems and controls. I improved the day-to-day reporting of KPI and enhanced[5] the level of detail in the EOY reports, making it easier for top-level[6] management to make strategic decisions. I also successfully reduced taxation costs for the company by 10 percent for the two years I was there.

I am meticulous, hard working, and have a special knowledge of British culture, as I lived and studied in Leicester for one year and took my ACCA there. I believe I am suitably qualified and experienced for the job advertised. I would be interested in talking with you further about what opportunities you have.

I look forward to hearing from you.

Yours sincerely,

Daisy Wang

Word List

1. oversee [ˋovɚˋsi] v. 監督
2. lead-up n. 準備階段
3. expedite [ˋɛkspɪˌdaɪt] v. 加速
4. overhaul [ˌovɚˋhɔl] v. 徹底檢查
5. enhance [ɪnˋhæns] v. 提高
6. top-level adj. 高階的

106 台北郵政信箱 765432
電話：0987 654 321
電子郵件：Daisy.Wang@notmail.com

本日日期

強尼・沃克先生
會計經理
KnowHow Inc.
台北市館前路 12 號 11 樓

敬愛的沃克先生：

　　本人於 2007 年 3 月 6 日自《財經時報》獲悉貴公司徵求會計主管一名，特來信應徵。

　　從所附的履歷表可得知本人為執業會計師與國際特許公認會計師會員，具有建立和審查財務控管，及仔細規畫稅務以成功節稅的實務經驗。

　　本人目前在 KPGM 擔任客戶服務經理與稅務顧問，至今已在此服務二年。本人的職務包括管理三個國際企業客戶在中華民國各個方面的稅務，其中有兩個客戶是在資訊科技業，另一個是在藥劑業。本人有興趣重拾和發展公司內部財務管理的經驗，尤其是在快速成長的工作環境中，況且本人在此方面已有相當經驗。

　　自 2003 至 2005 年，本人在 BonK 擔任財務部副理一職，期間 BonK 與 System Integrated Silica Controls 合併。在合併之前，本人主要負責財務部的日常運作，包括指導一個 15 人小組。本人亦搜集關於關鍵績效指標的資料和彙整管理報告，其中包括每月預測報告和準備提報有關編列年度預算的建議。此外，本人負責監督所有外部查帳審核的工作。在合併預備階段，本人幫助重新設計財

務系統控管，並參與合併後新公司的長期財務策略計畫。另外也曾與 SISC 的財務部合作，監督兩家公司的稅務整合工作，以加速合併後新公司的首次內部查帳審核事務。

　　自 2001 到 2003 年，本人為好不好塑膠公司的資深審計員，在該公司本人亦指導了一個包含 12 名財務人員的工作團隊。除了公司內部和外部的查帳審查，本人更大幅修改了公司的財務系統和控管。本人亦改善了日常的關鍵績效指標報告和提高了年終報告的詳盡度，讓高層主管能更輕鬆做出策略性決定。此外，本人在該公司任職的兩年期間，成功為公司減少一成的稅務成本。

　　本人個性謹慎細心、工作勤奮，並對英國文化尤其了解，因本人曾在英國的萊斯特居住和求學一年，本人的國際特許公認會計師會員資格即在該地取得。本人深具自信必能符合貴公司求才廣告中所列條件與必要經驗，期與貴公司進一步討論可能的工作機會。

　　靜候回音

王黛西　敬上

目標式求職信 4 ：職場老手篇

P.O.Box 765432 Taipei 106, Taiwan
Telephone: 0987 654 321
Email: Daisy.Wang@notmail.com

Month Day, Year

Ms. Calista Chen
Personnel Department
Jarndyce & Jarndyce
12 Guanqian Rd., 11th Floor Taipei 106, Taiwan

Dear Ms. Chen,

I am writing in connection with the advert for an international tax specialist in *The Economist* 6 March 2007.

You will see from my attached CV that I am a CPA and ACCA member with proven experience in providing individuals and corporations with innovative tax solutions. I have excellent client relations skills, and experience with utilizing international tax environments to make tax cost savings for my clients.

For the last two years I have been working as a client service manager and tax consultant with KPGM. My present position mainly involves managing ROC tax affairs in all areas of taxation for three international corporate clients with operations in Taiwan, two of whom are in the IT sector, and one in the pharmaceutical sector. I have been able to achieve average tax savings of 5 percent for all my clients within one year. In addition, I increased tax savings by 25 percent for one client in particular by utilizing loopholes in regional offshore tax regulations. I have been able to develop and maintain excellent relations with the new

CFO of one of my clients. This has resulted in increased business for my company.

From 1997 to 2000 I was an accounting clerk for Sunshine CPA in Taiwan. My duties there included advising foreign entrepreneurs setting up businesses in Taiwan. As well as advising them on all aspects of taxation, including employment tax, stamp duties, business tax, and capital gains, I also created bespoke financial systems for my corporate clients, in order to make their tax reporting process easier and more transparent.[1] I also advised on international tax planning needs for high net worth individuals.[2] I brought in five new clients for the company during my time there, largely through referrals[3] from existing clients, which increased company revenue by 32 percent.

From 2001 to 2005 I worked in-company for two major Taiwanese IT companies, where I led teams of finance personnel. I guided my teams in producing meticulous reports, and trained some of them for the local CPA test.

I am scrupulous, hard working, and proactive in taking care of my clients' needs. I am also keen to learn and develop new technical skills. I am currently in the final stages of my MBA, writing my thesis on international tax law, focusing on the Asia-Pacific Region. I believe I am suitably qualified and experienced for the job advertised. I would be interested in talking with you further about what opportunities you have.

I look forward to hearing from you.

Sincerely yours,

Daisy Wang
Daisy Wang

Word List
1. transparent [træns`pɛrənt] *adj.* 透明的
2. high net worth individual *n.* 高淨值人士
3. referral [rɪ`fɜəl] *n.* 推舉

106 台北郵政信箱 765432

電話： 0987 654 321

電子郵件： Daisy.Wang@notmail.com

本日日期

卡莉思塔‧陳女士
人事部門
Jarndyce & Jarndyce
台北市館前路 12 號 11 樓

敬愛的陳女士：

　　本人於 2007 年 3 月 6 日自《經濟學人》獲悉貴公司徵求國際稅務專員一名，特來信應徵。

　　從所附的履歷表可得知本人為執業會計師與國際特許公認會計師會員，具有提供企業和個人高所得報稅諮詢服務的實際經驗。本人具備絕佳的客戶關係技巧，以及曾利用國際稅制為客戶節稅的經驗。

　　在過去兩年當中，本人一直在 KPGM 擔任客戶服務經理與稅務顧問。目前的職位主要負責管理三個國際企業客戶在中華民國各個方面的稅務，其中有兩個客戶是在資訊科技業，另一個是在藥劑業。本人曾在一年內為所有客戶成功節省了 5% 的稅。此外，還曾利用地區性海外稅制的漏洞，特別為一個客戶額外節省了二成五的稅。本人與其中一個客戶新上任的首席財務長建立和維持極好的關係，也因此為公司帶來更高的收入。

　　從 1997 到 2000 年，本人在台灣陽光執業會計事務所擔任會計員一職，在此職務包括為在台灣設立公司的外國企業家提供各方面的稅務諮詢服務，包括就業稅、印花稅、營業稅和資本利得稅，本人亦為企業客戶建立了預設財務系統，讓客戶的報稅過程更加方便和透明。本人也為高淨值個人提供國際稅務規畫等方

面的諮詢服務。本人在此公司服務期間曾帶進五個新客戶，主要管道是透過現有客戶的推薦，更因而為公司增加了三成二的收入。

從 2001 到 2005 年，本人曾在台灣兩大資訊科技公司擔任公司的內部職位，在這兩家公司中均為領導財務人員的工作團隊。本人指導工作團隊製作出嚴謹的報告，並訓練部分成員參加當地的執業會計師執照考試。

本人個性謹慎細心、工作勤奮並積極滿足客戶需求，同時熱切希望學習和建立新的技術技能。目前正在攻讀商管碩士學位的最後階段，努力撰寫論文，論文是以國際稅法為題，並以研究亞太地區為主。本人自信必能符合貴公司求才廣告所列條件和必要經驗，期與貴公司進一步討論可能的工作機會。

靜候回音

王黛西　敬上

Task 2.4 ▶參考答案

請利用下表核對答案並閱讀後面的解析。

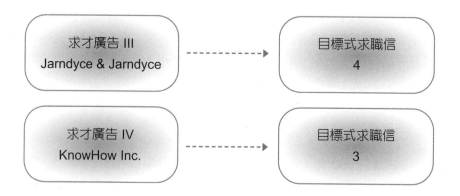

求職信解析

▶ 這兩封目標式求職信都有註明收信的對象。若能查出在公司握有面試決定權者的名字，各位的求職信便會看起來更加專業，獲得面試的機會也會提高。收件人的名字往往在求才廣告中便會提供，或上網從公司網站搜尋一下，通常也找得到。

▶ 收件人如爲男士請用 Mr.，女士則用 Ms.。若從對方名字看不出是男士還是女士，那麼就按照求才廣告或網站上的名字，全部拼寫出來，如 Dear Sankyu Watalotopor。

▶ 如果找不到或不確定對方名字，別擔心，就跟非目標式求職信一樣，寫 Dear Sir/Madam 即可。

▶ 要是求職信有特定的收件人，別忘了在信末以 Yours sincerely, 或 Sincerely yours, 結尾。

現在我們要來學習的是求職信的寫作架構。無論目標式或非目標式求職信，兩者的寫作架構都是一樣的。

Task 2.5

請回頭重新閱讀所有的求職信，研究其中的寫作架構，然後依序將下面方框中所列的各項架構名稱，寫在下方流程圖的步驟中。

- Current situation
- Introduction
- Statement of purpose
- Conclusion
- Work history

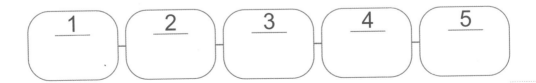

Task 2.5 ▶參考答案

請根據下面的求職信架構流程圖核對答案,並閱讀解析。

求職信架構解析

▶ 所有的求職信都有表明來信意圖。若為目標式求職信,說明來信意圖之時應該提及求才廣告;若為非目標式求職信,說明來信意圖之時則應該提及希望應徵的部門。

▶ 第二段主要是自我介紹技能和資歷。這一段應該要提到履歷表。在目標式求職信中,自我介紹時應該盡量重複運用求才廣告中的語彙,這樣求職信就會更顯得目標化。此外,應該提及你對求才廣告中描述的職務也有一些經驗;撰寫非目標式求職信時,這一段應該提到一些重點工作經驗,並告知對方接下來將以一、二段的篇幅說明這些經驗。這部分的寫作將於本單元稍後再行介紹。在自我介紹的段落中,應該以現在簡單式為主。

▶ 接下來的段落通常是描述自己目前的工作。若提到離開現職的原因,請將重點放在希望從下一份工作中學到什麼,而不要抱怨對現職的不滿。請盡量用數字呈現現職所做的具體貢獻。描述現在工作的職務時應用動詞現在進行式,描述為現任公司呈現的戰果時則應用動詞現在完成式。

▶ 第四部分的篇幅可以有一至二個段落長,主要描述過去的工作經驗,每一段落描述一份工作。這部分只能用動詞過去簡單式,此外,如果有的話,最好也用數字呈現業績實例。

▶ 最後一段應該描述的是個人特質,以及自認為是理想工作人選的理由。此時最好盡量重複運用求才廣告中的一些語彙。在非目標式求職信中,則應描述你自認會為團隊帶來貢獻的原因。也別忘了提及期待未來能和對方進一步連絡。

閱讀完以上解析,請回頭閱讀所有的求職信,確定解析中提到的各項須知都能明確認出。

求職達人基本功：關鍵動詞

現在我們繼續往下學習，深入研究求職信會用到的語彙。

Task 2.6

　　請將下面的 set-phrases 分類，根據 Task 2.5 求職信的架構順序，在各個 set-phrases 的旁邊寫上所屬的架構編號。見範例。

Among my duties in my previous job were Ving and Ving ...	4
At the moment I am working as a n.p.	
For the last two years I have been Ving ...	
From X to X I worked as a n.p. at n.p.	
I already have some experience with this.	2
I also have extensive experience with n.p.	
I am currently Ving ...	
I am interested in Ving ...	
I am writing in connection with n.p.	1
I am writing in the hope that you have a vacancy for a n.p. in your n.p.	
I am writing in the hope that you have a vacant position for a n.p. in your n.p.	
I believe I am suitably qualified and experienced for the job advertised.	
I believe I would be a suitable addition to your team.	5
I have been able to V ...	
I was able to V ...	
I would be interested in talking with you further about what opportunities you have.	
I would like to extend my experience of ...	
I would welcome the opportunity to talk with you further about what opportunities you have.	
I'm writing to apply for the position of n.p.	
My job here includes Ving ...	
My job there was to V ...	
My main duties were to V ...	
My present position involves Ving ...	
This has resulted in n.p.	3
While at n.p., my duties included Ving ...	
You will see from my attached CV that + clause.	

Task 2.6 ▶參考答案

請利用下面的必備語庫核對答案。

求職必備語庫 2.1

1. Statement of purpose

I am writing in connection with n.p.

I'm writing to apply for the position of n.p.

I am writing in the hope that you have a vacancy for a n.p. in your n.p.

I am writing in the hope that you have a vacant position for a n.p. in your n.p.

2. Introduction

You will see from my attached CV that + clause.

I also have extensive experience with n.p.

I already have some experience with this.

I am interested in Ving ...

I would like to extend my experience of n.p.

3. Current situation

I am currently Ving ...

At the moment I am working as a n.p.

For the last two years I have been Ving ...

My present position involves Ving ...

My job here includes Ving ...

I have been able to V ...

This has resulted in n.p.

4. Work history

While at n.p., my duties included Ving ...

I was able to V ...

From X to X I worked as a n.p. at n.p.

My job there was to V ...

My main duties were to V ...

Among my duties in my previous job were Ving and Ving ...

5. Conclusion

I believe I am suitably qualified and experienced for the job advertised.

I would welcome the opportunity to talk with you further about what opportunities you have.

I would be interested in talking with you further about what opportunities you have.

I believe I would be a suitable addition to your team.

Task　2.7

請回頭重新閱讀本單元的所有求職信，找出其中用到必備語庫 2.1 的 set-phrases，並畫上底線。此外，也要注意這些 set-phrases 的用法。

Task　2.8

請回頭重新閱讀前面幾封求職信，找出信中各個段落所使用的動詞時態，並畫上底線。若有屬於 set-phrases 的動詞則請略過，只須找出各段落中的其他動詞即可。

現在要來練習該如何運用這些 set-phrases。我們將側重在 (3) 的現況和 (4) 的工作經歷兩部分。記住，在描述現況的段落中，談到工作內容時應使用動詞進行式（如：be Ving、have been Ving），而談到工作成果時則應使用動詞完成式（have p.p.）。按：p.p. 即指過去分詞（past participle）。

Task 2.9

現在請根據自己現在的工作，完成以下造句。

- I am currently Ving ...

_____

- At the moment I am working as a n.p.

_____

- For the last two years I have been Ving ∴

_____

- My present position involves n.p./Ving ...

_____

- My job here includes n.p./Ving ...

_____

- I have been able to V ...

_____

- This has resulted in n.p.

_____

Task 2.9 ▶參考答案

以下提供一些範例答案。各位也可以利用 MP3 中的音檔練習這些句子的語調。

> ▶ I am currently completing my studies in finance administration.
> ▶ At the moment I am working as a sales assistant at Sogo.
> ▶ For the past two years I have been working as a tax officer at KPGM.
> ▶ My present position involves looking after clients.
> ▶ My job here includes sales and conducting after sales service.
> ▶ I have been able to increase revenue for the company by 3%.
> ▶ This has resulted in 3 more customers for the company.

Task 2.10

現在請根據各位過去的工作資歷，完成以下造句。

- While at n.p., my duties included n.p./Ving ...

_____

- I was able to V ...

_____

- From X to X I worked as a n.p. at n.p.

_____

- My job there was to V ...

_____

- My main duties were to V ...

_____

- Among my duties in my previous job were Ving and Ving ...

_____

Task　2.10　▶參考答案

以下提供一些範例答案。各位也可以利用 MP3 中的音檔練習這些句子的語調。

> ▶ While at Sogo, my duties included sales and conducting after sales service.
> ▶ I was able to bring in three more customers and increase revenue for the company by 16 percent.
> ▶ From 2001 to 2003 I worked as a sales assistant at Sogo.
> ▶ My job there was to assess client's credit ratings and file reports.
> ▶ My main duties were to answer the telephone and take inquiries.
> ▶ My main duties were to deal with customer complaints.
> ▶ Among my duties in my previous job were operating the cash register and taking money from the customers.

　　在求職信中，說明過去就職經驗的篇幅可能會是最長的部分，因此需要用到更多其他描述不同職務的動詞。故以下是一些用於凸顯不同商業職務和著重經驗中不同面向的動詞：

▶ 若想凸顯成功完成（completed successfully）的事件：
I increased revenue by 23 percent.
▶ 若希望凸顯解決問題（solved a problem）的成果：
I identified weaknesses with the customer database.
▶ 若想尋求較資深的職位，則可強調曾經如何管理一組團隊（managed people）：
I supervised a team of eight and delegated tasks to them.
▶ 若想強調團隊合作的特質，則可描述過去的合作經驗（worked with people）：
I collaborated on a DM with members from the marketing department.
▶ 若想凸顯自己曾有過處理財務（handled money）的經驗：
I balanced the books every month.
▶ 或想凸顯自己曾有過整理資料（handled data）的經驗：
I catalogued the customer inquiry records, making them easier to use.
▶ 或只是希望說明一個曾經經手的案子（worked on a project）：
I translated the company brochures from Chinese into English.

Task 2.11

請看下面 137 個常用的動詞，並分別寫在後面表格中所屬的欄位之一。

• Achieved sth. 完成；達成	• Audited sth. 審核	• Collected sth. 收集
• Addressed sth. 處理；滿足	• Authored sth. 開創；發起	• Compiled sth. 彙編
• Advised on sth. 建議	• Balanced sth. 平衡	• Consolidated sth. 鞏固
• Allocated sth. (to sth.) 分派；分配	• Brought in sth. 產生	• Consulted with sb. on sth.　商量
• Analyzed sth. 分析	• Budgeted sth. 編入預算	• Contracted sb. to V 簽約
• Anticipated sth. 預料	• Built up sth. 建起	• Convinced sb. to V 說服
• Appraised sth. 估價	• Calculated sth. 計算	• Coordinated with sb. to V　協調
• Approved sth. 批准	• Carried out sth. 完成；實行	• Corresponded with sb. about sth.　通信
• Arbitrated (between sth. and) sth.　仲裁	• Catalogued sth. 編入目錄	• Counseled sb. on sth. 輔導
• Arranged sth. 安排	• Chaired sth. 主持	• Created sth. 創造；設計
• Assembled sth. 召集	• Clarified sth. 闡明；澄清	• Customized sth. 訂做
• Assessed sth. 評估	• Classified sth. 分類	• Dealt with sth. 處理；應付
• Assisted in sth. 協助	• Coached sb. on sth. 指導	• Delegated sth. to sb. 委派
• Attained sth. 達到	• Collaborated on sth. with sb.　合作	• Demonstrated sth. 示範操作

- Designed sth.
  設計
- Developed sth.
  開發
- Diagnosed sth. as sth.
  診斷
- Directed sth.
  指導；指揮
- Drafted sth.
  起草
- Edited sth.
  編輯；校訂
- Engineered sth.
  設計；建造
- Enlisted sb. to V
  徵募
- Established sth.
  建立；制定
- Evaluated sth.
  估價；鑑定
- Examined sth.
  檢查；調查
- Executed sth.
  實施；執行
- Expedited sth.
  迅速執行
- Facilitated in sth.
  促進
- Forecasted sth.
  預測
- Focused on sth.
  著重；強調

- Formulated sth.
  規畫；想出
- Founded sth.
  建立
- Generated sth.
  造成；生產
- Guided sb.
  指導某人
- Had overall responsibility for sth.　全權負責
- Handled sth.
  操作；管理
- Identified sth.
  發現；確定
- Implemented sth.
  實施；執行
- Improved sth.
  改善；增進
- Increased sth. (by number)　提高
- Influenced sth.
  影響
- Initiated sth.
  創始
- Inspected sth.
  檢查；審查
- Instituted sth.
  創立；制定
- Integrated sth.
  合併
- Interviewed sb.
  面試

- Introduced sth. into sth.
  介紹
- Invented sth.
  發明
- Investigated sth.
  調查
- Kept up sth.
  保持
- Lectured on sth.
  演講
- Led sth.
  領導
- Listened to sb.
  聽從
- Maintained sth.
  保持
- Managed sth.
  管理；經營
- Marketed sth.
  （在市場上）銷售
- Mediated between X and Y　居中調解
- Moderated sth.
  減輕
- Motivated sb. to V
  激發
- Negotiated with sb. on
  就……與某人協商
- Negotiated sth.
  協商
- Operated sth.
  操作

- Organized sth.
  組織；安排
- Originated sth
  引起；產生
- Overhauled sth.
  大修
- Oversaw sth.
  監督；管理
- Performed sth.
  完成；執行
- Persuaded sb. to V
  說服
- Pioneered sth.
  開闢；倡導
- Planned sth.
  計畫；規畫
- Participated in sth.
  參加；參與
- Prepared sth. (for sb.)
  準備
- Presented sth. (to sb.)
  呈現
- Prioritized sth.
  優先處理
- Produced sth.
  製作；產出
- Programmed sth.
  制定計畫
- Projected sth.
  企劃；計畫
- Promoted sth.
  促進；創立

- Publicized sth.
  宣傳
- Recommended sth.
  推薦
- Recruited sb.
  吸收；招募
- Reduced sth. (by number)　降低
- Rehabilitated sth.
  恢復
- Remolded sth.
  重新塑造
- Reorganized sth.
  整頓；重新制定
- Repaired sth.
  修理
- Reported sth.
  報告
- Represented sth.
  代表
- Researched sth.
  調查；探究
- Resolved sth.
  解決
- Reviewed sth.
  複審
- Revitalized sth.
  恢復
- Scheduled sth.
  安排；預定
- Set up sth.
  建造；創造

- Shaped sth.
  計畫；設計
- Sold sth.
  賣出
- Solved sth.
  解決
- Spearheaded sth.
  帶頭
- Strengthened sth.
  加強
- Supervised sth.
  監督
- Systematized sth.
  系統化
- Taught sb.
  傳授
- Took care of sth.
  處理
- Trained sb.
  訓練
- Translated sth.
  翻譯
- Upgraded sth.
  升級
- (was) Responsible for sth.　負責
- Worked on sth.
  做
- Wrote sth.
  撰寫

1. Completed successfully

2. Solved a problem

3. Managed people

4. Worked with people

5. Handled money

6. Handled data

7. Worked on a project

Task **2.11** ▶參考答案

請利用必備語庫 2.2 核對答案，並閱讀語庫解析。

求職必備語庫 2.2

1. Completed successfully	
Achieved sth.	Instituted sth.
Attained sth.	Negotiated sth.
Brought in sth.	Organized sth.
Built up sth.	Originated sth.
Consolidated sth.	Pioneered sth.
Created sth.	Produced sth.
Established sth.	Programmed sth.
Executed sth.	Reduced sth. (by number)
Expedited sth.	Revitalized sth.
Founded sth.	Set up sth.
Generated sth.	Shaped sth.
Improved sth.	Sold sth.
Increased sth. (by number)	Spearheaded sth.
Influenced sth.	Strengthened sth.
Initiated sth.	Systematized sth.

2. Solved a problem	
Addressed sth.	Remolded sth.
Diagnosed sth. as sth.	Reorganized sth.
Evaluated sth.	Repaired sth.
Examined sth.	Resolved sth.
Identified sth.	Reviewed sth.
Improved sth.	Revitalized sth.
Investigated sth.	Solved sth.
Overhauled sth.	Strengthened sth.
Reduced sth. (by number)	Upgraded sth.
Rehabilitated sth.	

3. Managed people

Appraised sth.	Managed sth.
Arbitrated (between sth. and) sth.	Mediated between X and Y
Chaired sth.	Moderated sth.
Coached sb. on sth.	Motivated sb. to V
Counseled sb. on sth.	Oversaw sth.
Delegated sth. to sb.	Recruited sb.
Directed sth.	Supervised sth.
Guided sb.	Taught sb.
Had overall responsibility for sth.	Trained sb.
Interviewed sb.	(was) Responsible for sth.
Lectured on sth.	Enlisted sb. to V
Led sth.	

4. Worked with people

Advised on sth.	Corresponded with sb. about sth.
Assisted in sth.	Listened to sb.
Collaborated on sth. with sb.	Negotiated with sb. on
Consulted with sb. on sth.	Persuaded sb. to V
Contracted sb. to V	Participated in sth.
Convinced sb. to V	Facilitated in sth.
Coordinated with sb. to V	

5. Handled money

Allocated sth. (to sth.)	Calculated sth.
Audited sth.	Forecasted sth.
Balanced sth.	Projected sth.
Budgeted sth.	

6. Handled data	
Analyzed sth.	Compiled sth.
Catalogued sth.	Formulated sth.
Clarified sth.	Prioritized sth.
Classified sth.	Projected sth.
Collected sth.	Researched sth.

7. Worked on a project		
Anticipated sth.	Engineered sth.	Prepared sth. (for sb.)
Approved sth.	Focused on sth.	Presented sth. to sb.
Arranged sth.	Handled sth.	Prioritized sth.
Assembled sth.	Implemented sth.	Promoted sth.
Assessed sth.	Inspected sth.	Publicized sth.
Authored sth.	Integrated sth.	Recommended sth.
Carried out sth.	Introduced sth. into sth.	Reported sth.
Customized sth.	Invented sth.	Represented sth.
Dealt with sth.	Kept up sth.	Scheduled sth.
Demonstrated sth.	Maintained sth.	Took care of sth.
Designed sth.	Marketed sth.	Translated sth.
Developed sth.	Operated sth.	Worked on sth.
Drafted sth.	Performed sth.	Wrote sth.
Edited sth.	Planned sth.	

語庫解析

▶ 上表所有的動詞都是用過去簡單式，這是因為在求職信中這些動詞是適用於描述工作資歷的部分。

▶ 其中有的動詞可能會出現在多個類別當中，因為這個表的分類規定並非硬性界定，而是作為各位使用時的參考法則，幫助各位選出適合的動詞，適切凸顯資歷中的不同面向。

▶ 各位在撰寫履歷表時也可使用這些動詞。

Task **2.12**

現在請回頭閱讀本單元的求職信和上一單元的履歷表，找出以上這些動詞並畫上底線，然後仔細研究這些動詞的用法。

好，現在我們要來學的是如何變換句子結構，好留給對方英語能力優異的印象。所以接下來要介紹給各位的是，如何補充之前已經提過的重點。

Task **2.13**

請看下面兩組句子，這兩組句子有何相同和不同之處？

- I had control of a large budget and was responsible for setting sales targets for the regional sales force.

- I had control of a large budget. In addition, I was responsible for setting sales targets for the regional sales force.

Task **2.13** ▶ 參考答案

希望各位能夠看出這兩組句子所要傳達的資訊其實是一樣的，重點有二：他或她有能力控管龐大的預算和設定售貨目標。

不過在第一組句子當中，資訊是合併成一個句子，而第二組的句子則是分成兩句來寫。

現在讓我們再來看看這兩種寫法可能用到的用語。

Task 2.14

請閱讀必備語庫 2.3 和下面的例句。

求職必備語庫 2.3

Linking two clauses	Linking two sentences
... and ...	At the same time, ...
... also ...	Apart from this, ...
... and also ...	As well as this, ...
... both n.p./Ving/clause and n.p./Ving/clause.	In addition, ...
... as well as n.p./Ving ...	In addition to this, ...

- I had control of a large budget and also was responsible for setting sales targets for the regional sales force.
- I had control of both a large budget and setting sales targets for the regional sales force.
- I had control of a large budget as well as setting sales targets for the regional sales force.
- I had control of a large budget. Apart from this, I was responsible for setting sales targets for the regional sales force.
- I had control of a large budget. At the same time, I was responsible for setting sales targets for the regional sales force.
- I had control of a large budget. As well as this, I was responsible for setting sales targets for the regional sales force.

━━━語庫小叮嚀
- 若連接詞是用來連接兩個子句,第二個子句的動詞不須重複主詞,因為兩個子句的主詞都是 I。
- 但若連接詞是用來連接兩個句子,則第二個句子的動詞一定要有主詞。
- 此外,標點符號一定要準確。

Task 2.15

現在請改寫以上必備語庫的例句,將兩個子句的改成兩個句子,兩個句子的則合併成兩個子句。

Task 2.16

請回去看在 Task 2.9 和 2.10 中所造的句子,用連接詞合併至少其中兩個句子。可參見以下範例。

• I am currently completing my studies in finance administration. At the same time, I am working as a sales assistant at Sogo.
• I am currently completing my studies in finance administration as well as working as a sales assistant at Sogo.

• My main duties were to both answer the telephone and take inquiries and deal with customer complaints.
• My main duties were to answer the telephone and take inquiries. As well as this, I also had to deal with customer complaints.

 求職達人基本功：詞彙應用（二）

在上一單元中，我們研究過如何在 CV 的個人簡介中重複使用求才廣告中的語彙，以使 CV 更加目標化。在結束本單元的學習之前，我們還要來研究如何在求職信中重複使用求才廣告中的語彙，同樣地讓求職信更加目標化。

Task 2.17

請完成下表。有哪些求才廣告和 CV 中的語彙也出現在求職信中呢？注意這些語彙的用法，以使求職信更加目標化。

	求才廣告 I	目標式 CV 2	目標式 求職信 2
Sales	✓	✓	
Logistics	✓	✓	
Technical	✓	✓	
Excited by opportunities	✓	-	
Career development	✓	-	
Motivated by the challenge	✓	-	
Learning new skills	✓	-	
Inventory management	✓	✓	
	求才廣告 II	目標式 CV 1	目標式 求職信 1
Creative input	✓	-	
Managing customer inquiries	✓	✓	
Marketing event management	✓	-	
Selling	✓	-	
Budget management	✓	✓	

Task　2.17 ▶參考答案

請利用下表核對答案，並閱讀語彙解析。

	求才廣告 I	目標式 CV 2	目標式 求職信 2
Sales	✓	✓	✓
Logistics	✓	✓	✓
Technical	✓	✓	✓
Excited by opportunities	✓	-	✓
Career development	✓	-	✓
Motivated by the challenge	✓	-	✓
Learning new skills	✓	-	✓
Inventory management	✓	✓	✓
	求才廣告 II	目標式 CV 1	目標式 求職信 1
Creative input	✓	-	✓
Managing customer inquiries	✓	✓	✓
Marketing event management	✓	-	✓
Selling	✓	-	✓
Budget management	✓	✓	✓

語彙解析

▶ 可以重複使用求才廣告的語彙，如此一來，求職信不僅顯得更加目標化，也可連帶達到求職信和履歷表相呼應的效果。

▶ 這些寫法都可幫各位將爭取到面試的機會提升，因為各位懂得如何把自己塑造得更像理想人選。

▶ 此外，在求職信中，這些語彙很多都出現在自我介紹和結論的段落中。

▶ 也請注意一些些微的變化。例如在求才廣告 I 中是說 motivated by the challenge of constantly learning...，但在求職信中則說 motivated by challenges，後者的意思比較攏統。

▶ 各位可以利用這類些微的變換，讓語彙更加貼切，以符合你的個人經驗。

Task 2.18

請完成下表。有哪些求才廣告和 CV 中的語彙也出現在求職信中呢？注意這些語彙的用法，以使求職信更目標化。

	求才廣告 III	目標式 CV 4	目標式 求職信 4
International tax planning	✓	✓	
Individuals and corporations	✓	✓	
Employer contributions	✓	✓	
Capital gains	✓	✓	
Stamp duty	✓	✓	
Tax solutions	✓	-	
Excellent client relations	✓	✓	
Keen to learn and develop new technical skills	✓	-	
	求才廣告 IV	目標式 CV 3	目標式 求職信 3
Review and development of system controls	✓	✓	
Financial strategic planning	✓	✓	
Tax planning	✓	✓	
Cost reduction	✓	✓	
External auditing	✓	-	
Internal auditing	✓	-	

Task 2.18 ▶參考答案

請利用下表核對答案，並閱讀語彙解析。

	求才廣告 III	目標式 CV 4	目標式 求職信 4
International tax planning	✓	✓	-
Individuals and corporations	✓	✓	✓
Employer contributions	✓	✓	✓
Capital gains	✓	✓	-
Stamp duty	✓	✓	-
Tax solutions	✓	-	✓
Excellent client relations	✓	✓	✓
Keen to learn and develop new technical skills	✓	-	✓
	求才廣告 IV	目標式 CV 3	目標式 求職信 3
Review and development of system controls	✓	✓	✓
Financial strategic planning	✓	✓	✓
Tax planning	✓	✓	✓
Cost reduction	✓	✓	✓
External auditing	✓	-	✓
Internal auditing	✓	-	✓

語彙解析

▶ 可以重複使用求才廣告中的語彙，如此一來，求職信不僅顯得更加目標化，也可連帶達到求職信和履歷表相互呼應的效果。

▶ 這些寫法都可幫助各位將爭取到面試的機會提升，因為各位懂得如何把自己塑造得更像理想人選。

▶ 此外，在求職信中，這些語彙很多都出現在自我介紹和結論的篇幅中。

▶ 也請注意一些些微的變化。例如在求才廣告 III 中是說 excellent client relations...，但在求職信中則說 excellent customer relation skills，兩者的意思大致上是相同的。

▶ 各位可以利用這類些微的變換，讓語彙更加貼切，以符合你的個人經驗。

Task 2.19

現在請針對某個想應徵的求才廣告,練習寫出一篇目標式求職信。並請盡量運用本單元所學到的寫作技巧。

好,本書的寫作篇到此結束。在繼續往下閱讀 Part 2 的準備面試之前,請先回到本單元前面的學習目標清單,確認是否每項目標都確實達成了。

Part 2

求職面試篇

 # 面試成功的準備和應對訣竅

恭喜你！你的 CV 和求職信達成目的，對方已經邀請你去面試了。

老實說，在面試開始不到兩分鐘，絕大多數人其實就已經定生死了。第一印象確實不容小覷，外表也相當重要。面試是各位展露光芒的機會，讓面試官知道無論工作或英文能力你都是佼佼者。由於機會只有一次，為面試做好萬全準備是絕對不容忽視的工作。準備充分時，便會更有自信展現出自己最好的一面。

在本節中將為各位介紹一些通用守則，為面試做好準備，同時也提供一些關於面試的一般須知。

● 面試之前：知彼

☐ 盡可能了解所應徵的工作。這份工作有什麼條件？有哪些挑戰？工作地點會在何處？需要多久出差一次？你能勝任這份工作嗎？你的上司是誰？你將會是獨立作業還是團隊工作？薪資多少？有哪些福利和規定？

☐ 盡可能了解所應徵的公司。公司的主要產品是什麼？主要市場為何？公司有什麼樣的文化？公司的創立歷史為何？公司是否剛完成合併或併購計畫？是否正準備執行合併或併購計畫？公司的國際知名度如何？這些資訊在求才廣告中應該都有提供，不過最好多下一點功夫做好背景研究。用 Google 搜尋一些相關文章，以了解這家公司目前所面對的課題。如果可以的話，和該公司的員工談一談。

☐ 盡可能了解該公司的主要市場。那是哪一類市場？這市場正在萎縮還是成長？市場可能受到哪些首要挑戰的影響，例如經濟或政府等因素？公司在市場上有哪些主要競爭對手？公司的市場占有率為何？目前的市場趨勢為何？

☐ 各位在應徵這份工作之前多半已在這行業待了很久，或者對產業已有所研究，因此對這個行業的脈動應已瞭若指掌，不過還是提醒各位要注意這個行業在當地環境的現況。

❑ 有哪些問題想問面試官？記住，面試是雙向的溝通，既是對方了解你的機會，也是你了解對方的機會，因此把想了解的問題列出來，到時對方也會以你所提問題的水準當作評斷的依據。思考一下哪些問題最能讓面試官對你刮目相看，或許那些問題你早已知道答案，但最好還是讓面試官知道你問得出高水準的問題。

❑ 千萬不要劈頭就問對方薪資或休假天數！第一次面試時很少人會談到條件和規定，這些事通常都是留待第二次面試時才會討論，或是透過電子郵件討論。

❑ 確定以上這些議題你都可以用英文侃侃而談。在 Unit 3 中，將向各位介紹如何準備一些實用的詞彙來談論這類議題。

● 面試之前：知己

❑ 確定自己可以談論目前工作相關的資訊，包括所採用的程序和系統、上司或下屬是誰，還有公司及部門的組織架構。

❑ 確定自己可以談論目前工作的滿意和不滿意之處，因為面試官會想知道各位離職的原因。但不要對目前工作有太多負面的批評，以免面試官覺得你是個麻煩人物。

❑ 在談論自己的時候最好保持謙遜的態度。各位能夠描述自己的長處和弱點嗎？

❑ 能夠談論自己對未來生涯的期望。各位希望學到什麼專業知識嗎？或希望補充經驗中哪些不足之處？

❑ 能夠談論自己對所應徵工作的期望。各位希望的薪資和福利為何？可先研究一下公司內部、行業中和市場上的一般薪資和福利水準。對薪資不要抱有不切實際的期待。雖然各位不必壓低姿態，但也不要要求太高。

❑ 確定自己的發音清晰，可以針對以上議題侃侃而談。在 Unit 4 中，將向各位介紹這部分的口說技巧。

● 面試當時：臨場表現

☐ 不要遲到。提早在面試前 10 分鐘報到，搭乘計程車赴會，既可避免報到時顯露出汗流浹背的窘態，也省去開車或騎機車還得擔心找不到停車位的麻煩。如果太早到，可以在附近散一散步，整理思緒。但千萬不要遲到。

☐ 衣著要得體。切記，第一印象其實比一般人想的還要來得重要。

☐ 如果是女性，最好穿著套裝和燙好的白色女衫，並搭配絲襪和矮跟女鞋。不要戴垂墜式的耳環。在面試前一天做好頭髮，但不要盤起來。化一點淡妝，讓自己看起來有自信即可，千萬不要一付濃妝豔抹要去狂歡的模樣。也不要珠光寶氣或擦太多香水。盡量看起來專業和保守，避免花枝招展或太過時髦的裝扮。

☐ 如果是男性，則應該穿西裝配白色襯衫和深色領帶。襯衫別忘了要燙平，鞋子應該擦亮，頭髮要梳洗，鬍子也得刮乾淨。面試前幾天去理個頭髮。盡量看起來專業和保守，避免太過華麗或時髦的裝扮。

☐ 把手機關掉。確定真的關掉，而不只是把鈴聲關掉而已。手機一定要關機，面試時受到干擾可不是各位所樂見的吧？

☐ 面試之前嚼一下口香糖保持口氣清新，但不要在面試時一邊嚼著口香糖，進入辦公大樓時就請先吐掉。

☐ 面試前的午餐不要吃大蒜或生蔥。

☐ 把當初寄給公司、幫你爭取到面試機會的履歷影本和求職信一併帶去，帶兩份放在透明的資料夾中，並攜帶一個款式保守但具專業形象的公事包。但不要把目前工作的名片也帶去了。

☐ 如果對方問起是否要喝飲料，請回答白開水就好。除非面試官也在喝，否則不要要求喝咖啡或茶。把杯子遠遠地放在面前的桌上，不要阻礙到雙方的互動，但也不要真的拿起來喝，以免一緊張而打翻，可就不妙了。面試之前和當時都不要吸菸（否則會有菸味）。

☐ 完整回答對方的問題，並提供許多實例，但避免露出輕浮的態度。態度一定要保持正向，即使討厭目前的工作也不要出口批評，以免給面試官留下不好的印象。

☐ 回答問題時不要僅說 yes 或 no。盡可能把答案講得清楚完整，並以過去工作經驗提供實際的例子。

☐ 語氣堅定而清楚。不要輕聲細語或細聲細氣，否則會給人膽小怕生的印象。呼吸順暢，面帶微笑且態度友善。就算緊張也不要表現出來，但也不要顯得過度自信。面試官講笑話時要禮貌地以笑回應，但自己則不要講笑話。

☐ 向對方提出問題。最好在面試結束之時，能讓面試官清楚明白你會是什麼樣的員工，以及你想不想要這份工作。

● 面試之後：評估

☐ 在面試的第二天寫一封電子郵件給面試官，感謝對方給予面試機會。簡短提到面試時所討論的話題，然後表示希望很快能得到回音。在附錄中已附上電子郵件的範例供各位參考。接下來就靜待對方的消息吧。

☐ 如果幾天後對方還是沒有消息，這大概就表示你沒有得到這份工作。千萬不要死纏爛打，如果對方要僱用你，就一定會和你連絡。

☐ 如果未能幸而中選，這是由於各位和這份工作要求的條件不完全符合，而非由於面試表現不佳而功敗垂成。別把這件事放在心上，也不要因此打擊了信心。

☐ 如果應徵未能成功，就把這次經驗當做練習面試技巧的一個機會吧。

Unit ③

準備面試
Before the Interview

引言與學習目標

　　在本單元中我們要學的是準備面試的方法。為面試做好萬全準備非常重要，因為這不單是各位第一次向雇主表現的機會，也可能是僅有的一次機會。所以，面試前應該要準備一些可能會用到的語彙與談話內容。一旦準備妥當，便會因而感到信心滿滿，爭取到工作的機會也會大為增加，因為絕大多數的人事面試官要找的不僅是能夠以公司語彙溝通的人，還要能瞭解公司和業界動態，且能用英文清楚準確地表達想法的人。要達到這些標準，最好的方法正是 word partnerships 的運用。 Word partnerships 就是代表各位的想法，因此準備時學會的 word partnerships 和在面試中用到的 word partnerships 越多，各位就越能表現出好口才和豐富的知識，也越能掌握應徵工作的相關議題、公司面臨的問題和業界遇到的一般議題，面試官對各位也就更加刮目相看了。

　　首先我們要來學習為面試準備 word partnerships 的訣竅，然後再學習為面試準備常見問題的答案。

　　本單元的學習結束之時，各位應該達成的學習目標：

❏ 學會準備 word partnerships 的方法，可針對所應徵的工作侃侃而談。
❏ 學會準備 word partnerships 的方法，可就面試公司和該公司所從事的產業侃侃而談。
❏ 知道面試中可能會問到的一些問題，並將這些問題的答案準備就緒。
❏ 學會一些可在面試中派上用場的關鍵詞彙。

準備領域或產業的專門字彙

接下來就以兩個情境來當作學習範例。在第一個情境中，要研究的是凱文如何爲面試準備一些可能會用到的語彙。在第二個情境中，則是以黛西爲研究對象。

專門字彙：職場新手篇

凱文最近看到通用汽車中國分公司的求才廣告，覺得自己很適合這份工作。他把目標式 CV 和求職信遞給該公司，也接到面試邀請函了。凱文爲準備面試，先是回去重新閱讀求才廣告，將裡面的詞彙仔細研究了一番。通用汽車中國分公司的求才廣告如下。

Task 3.1

請閱讀這份求才廣告，找出 word partnerships 並畫上底線。

Generally Great Motors (China) Ltd.
Location: Shanghai, China
Business Account Assistant Manager Job ID: B12345

Generally Great Motors is expanding rapidly in China. Generally Great Motors's focus in China is to grow the emerging[1] luxury car market and to establish GGM as the market leader in this segment in the long term. Current strategy focuses on creating new channels, especially in the new hypermarket[2] and supermarket channels, and in developing car care and after sales service to add value for the customer, helping to make GGM products the vehicle of preference for China's emerging, affluent[3] middle classes.

Responsibilities:

▸ Assist the account manager with the following duties:

▸ Responsible for the development of car care sales in modern trade outlets (hypermarket, supermarket, Internet, etc.)

 Word List

1. emerge [ɪˋmɝdʒ] *v.* 出現
2. hypermarket [ˋhaɪpəˌmɑrkɪt] *n.* 量販店
3. affluent [ˋæfluənt] *adj.* 富裕的

- ▶ Responsible for listing in targeted outlets and pushing sales through
- ▶ Develop marketing plan for car care sales in modern trade
- ▶ Develop promotion plan for targeted hypermarkets
- ▶ Deliver respective sales targets and collect revenues
- ▶ Gather market intelligence
- ▶ Submit business reports

Requirements:

- ▶ Bachelor's degree
- ▶ Fluent in English
- ▶ Ample[4] experience in dealing with modern trade
- ▶ Self motivated, responsible, strong sense of ownership[5]

通用汽車（中國）
工作地點：中國上海
商業帳戶協理 職位編碼： **B12345**

　　通用汽車在中國大陸正快速擴展。通用汽車在中國大陸的重點業務將是發展新興的豪華汽車市場，並在長遠的將來將公司打造成此區塊的市場領導者。目前策略是以開發新通路為重，尤其是在量販店和超級市場，以及開發汽車保養和售後服務等業務，以提供客戶更多附加價值，進而讓公司的產品成為中國新興富裕中產階級的代步工具。

工作內容：

- ▶ 協助帳戶經理從事以下職務：
- ▶ 負責在現代暢貨中心（量販店、超級市場和網路等）開發銷售汽車保養業務
- ▶ 負責在目標暢貨中心上市和推動業績
- ▶ 規畫現代貿易中汽車保養業務的行銷計畫
- ▶ 規畫在目標量販店的促銷計畫
- ▶ 達到各項業績目標和收款
- ▶ 收集市場情報
- ▶ 提交商業報告

Word List

4. ample [ˈæmp!] *adj.* 豐富的

5. sense of ownership *n.* 自主

須具備資格：
▶ 學士學位
▶ 英文流利
▶ 處理現代貿易的經驗豐富
▶ 自我激勵、負責、自主

Task 3.2

現在請利用上面求才廣告的詞彙，填寫下面的 word partnerships 表。見範例。

V	Adj.	N
expand	*rapidly*	—
grow	*emerging luxury*	*car market*
	market	
	new	
		care
		service
		—
—		
responsible for		sales
	targeted	
develop		plan
	promotion	
deliver		sales targets
collect	—	
		intelligence
		reports

Task 3.1 和 3.2 ▶參考答案

　　如果不熟這個領域，不要擔心，在此只是要介紹各位如何利用想應徵的求才廣告，建立與工作本身和公司有關的 word partnerships。請用下表核對答案。

　　請注意，形容詞那一欄中也含有一些名詞。因為有時 word partnerships 中會有兩個以上的名詞，這些名詞的功用就跟形容詞一樣，可以為第二個名詞補充資訊。各位只要知道 word partnership 中的所有字都是意義字即可，這一點在前言中介紹 Leximodel 和 word partnerships 時就已提過。

　　別忘了花時間背誦已學過的詞彙和練習發音。可利用一本附有光碟的好用字典，查出詞彙的發音，或反複聆聽本書所附的 MP3。

V	Adj./Adv.	N
expand	rapidly	—
grow	emerging luxury	car market
establish GGM as	market	leader
create	new	channels
develop	car	care
develop	after-sales	service
add	value	—
—	emerging, affluent	middle classes
responsible for	car care	sales
list in	targeted	outlets
develop	marketing	plan
develop	promotion	plan
deliver	respective	sales targets
collect	—	revenues
gather	market	intelligence
submit	business	reports

Task **3.3**

　　凱文後來在面試中用了以下句子談論與工作本身和公司相關的問題，請研究一下這些句子，並可利用 MP3 練習聽和說。

- I learned how to gather market intelligence and submit a business report in my business writing class in college. I managed to get good grades for that assignment.
- I think it's important to always create new channels for selling things to keep a competitive edge.
- I think I have some good ideas about how to develop after-sales service, as I have a good imagination and can understand people's needs. I also really like cars!

Task **3.3** ▶參考答案

　　在下一單元中將會爲各位介紹如何造出這類句子，現在各位只需了解凱文如何在面試中運用那些從求才廣告中蒐集到的詞彙，表現出他對工作相關問題的充分掌握，以及討論這些問題的口才。

　　以下是凱文前面所用句子的中文翻譯，供各位參考：

- 在大學的商業寫作課程中，我學到了收集市場情報和提交商業報告。我那次的作業取得了好成績。
- 我認爲不斷地開發新的銷售管道，以保持競爭優勢很重要。
- 我對如何建立售後服務有一些想法，因爲我想像力豐富，能夠了解一般人的需求。我也非常喜歡車子！

　　現在要介紹的是公司所面臨的宏觀問題、主要市場和業界的整體狀況。首先來看一看凱文如何準備可以用來討論這些大範圍問題的 word partnerships。他上網用 Google 查詢 "GGM China"，找到以下這篇討論該公司在中國面臨何種問題的文章。

Task 3.4

請閱讀這篇文章和譯文，然後回答下面問題。並可利用 MP3 練習聽力。

1. 何種因素刺激了中國高級汽車市場的成長？
2. 進口外國高級汽車市場是由哪幾家外商公司主導？
3. 國產外國高級汽車市場是由哪幾家外商公司主導？
4. 有哪些外商公司計畫進軍國產外國高級汽車市場？

China's luxury car market opens its doors

SHANGHAI — Ten years ago, most luxury cars were owned by government organizations or enterprises, but now more individuals are beginning to buy limousines. With over twenty years of reform and opening-up, China has created numerous millionaires and several billionaires. Last year at an auto show in Beijing, a Bentley was sold to an anonymous Chinese buyer for RMB¥8.88 million (US$1.07 million).

Official statistics show over ten million cars are privately owned in China. As living standards improve, consumers become more selective in purchasing cars. In the capital, many leading limousine brands can be seen, many of which are privately owned.

With the dramatically increasing number of wealthy Chinese, overseas auto giants are optimistic about the prospects of the Chinese market. They will make efforts to increase exports to China and expand local production of new models, experts say.

Joachim Ribben, executive director of Audi China, said the Chinese market was maturing as market divisions have become increasingly clear. The newly prosperous social class in China wants to demonstrate its success, offering an enormous potential market for luxury cars.

Audi has, to date, had a monopoly on luxury car production in China, but now it is preparing for increasingly heated competition with the local production of A4s this year. It began to import its A8 series to China to challenge the imported limousine market domination by Mercedes-Benz and BMW.

American-based auto giant Generally Great Motors will soon see its Series 3 sedans roll off the production line in northeast China's Liaoning Province, making it the second foreign luxury auto maker in China following Audi.

In addition to Audi and GGM, Japan's Toyota Motor Corporation plans to invest US$311 million to produce its luxury Crown model in China. The production of the Crown will be Toyota's first luxury car production outside Japan.

中國高級汽車市場大開門戶

【上海報導】十年前，大部分的豪華汽車都是政府機關或大企業的特權，不過現在已有越來越多的平民百姓也開始購買豪華大轎車了。經過二十多年來的改革和開放，中國已出現為數可觀的百萬富翁和不少億萬富翁。去年在北京的汽車展中，有一部賓特利便是以 888 萬元（約 107 萬美元）賣給一位不知名的中國買家。

官方統計顯示，在中國有一千萬輛私人汽車。當生活水準越來越高，大家買車時也就更加精挑細選。在首都的大街上隨處可見知名品牌的豪華轎車，其中不少皆為私人所有。

由於中國富裕人口劇增，國外的汽車大廠對中國市場的展望，無不抱持著樂觀的看法，據專家所說，這些汽車大廠勢必會努力提高對中國的進口量，同時擴大國產新車款的生產量。

奧迪中國分公司的執行長阿希姆．里賓表示，由於市場區隔越來越清楚，現在的中國市場可說是已趨成熟。中國新興的富裕社會階層需要展現自己物質上的成就，因而為豪華汽車市場帶來了可觀的成長能量。

目前奧迪獨占了中國豪華汽車生產市場，但是今年他們在當地生產的 A4 車款便得準備迎戰越來越激烈的競爭。他們已開始將 A8 車系引進中國，挑戰進口豪華汽車市場中的霸主賓士和朋馳。

來自美國的汽車大廠通用汽車位於中國東北遼寧省的工廠也即將推出第三車系的轎車，屆時通用汽車將晉升為繼奧迪之後在中國的第二大外國豪華汽車製造商。

除了奧迪和通用汽車，日本的豐田汽車公司也準備在中國斥資 3 億 1,110 萬美元生產豪華「皇冠」車款，這將會是豐田首次在日本本土以外展開的汽車生產計畫。

Task 3.4 ▶參考答案

1. 豪華汽車市場一片長紅的原因在於中國經濟開放了，購買進口豪華汽車以展現財富的中國富人也與日俱增。
2. 賓士和朋馳是進口汽車市場中的長年霸主。
3. 奧迪在中國生產外國品牌的汽車，他們是這種國產外國豪華汽車市場的長年霸主。
4. 通用汽車和豐田汽車都計畫在近期內開始在當地生產自家的車款，攻佔中國市場。

現在我們來看凱文如何利用這篇文章，建立用來談論所應徵公司、領域和業界的相關詞彙。

Task 3.5

請利用上面文章中的詞彙填寫下面的 word partnerships 表格。見範例。

V	Adj./Adv.	N
be owned by	*government*	*organizations*
buy	—	*limousines*
create		
—		show
be sold to		Chinese buyer
	living	
	more selective	—
—		limousine brands
—	privately ...	—
—	dramatically increasing	
—		auto giants
make	—	
increase	—	
expand		
—	market	
—		social class
	—	success
	enormous	
—	luxury	
	—	a monopoly (on)
—	luxury car	
prepare for		competition
	imported limousine	market domination
roll off	—	
making (it)	second foreign luxury	
	—	US$311 million

Task　3.5　▶參考答案

　　請利用下表核對答案。若因領域不同而有很多詞彙不懂，也沒有關係。從這個習題可以訓練各位從文章中找出 word partnerships 的能力。

　　相信各位已經注意到並非所有的 word partnerships 都有形容詞或動詞。

V	Adj./Adv.	N
be owned by	government	organizations
buy	—	limousines
create	numerous	millionaires
—	auto	show
be sold to	anonymous	Chinese buyer
improve	living	standards
become	more selective	—
—	leading	limousine brands
—	privately owned	—
—	dramatically increasing	number (of)
—	overseas	auto giants
make	—	efforts
increase	—	exports
expand	local	production
—	market	divisions
—	newly prosperous	social class
demonstrate	—	success
offer	enormous	potential market
—	luxury	cars
have	—	a monopoly (on)
—	luxury car	production
prepare for	increasingly heated	competition
challenge	imported limousine	market domination
roll off	—	production line
making (it)	second foreign luxury	auto maker
plans to invest	—	US$311 million

Task 3.6

凱文在面試中用了以下句子談論通用汽車在中國所面對的問題,請研究一下這些句子,並可利用 MP3 練習聽和說。

> • Because the Chinese economy is creating numerous millionaires, it's important to make efforts to keep their loyalty once they make their purchase.
> • I think there is an enormous potential market for after-sales service for luxury cars. That's one way for us to prepare for the increasingly heated competition from other overseas auto giants.

Task 3.6 ▶參考答案

在下一單元中將會為各位介紹如何造出這類句子。現在各位只需了解凱文如何在面試中運用那些從文章中蒐集到的詞彙,表現出他對公司和業界相關議題的充分掌握,以及討論這些議題的專業內涵和口才。

以下是凱文上面所用句子的中文翻譯,供各位參考:

> • 由於中國的經濟造就的百萬富翁人數可觀,在這些人購買了產品以後,努力維持他們對產品的忠誠度是很重要的。
> • 外國汽車大廠的競爭日益激烈,我認為豪華汽車售後服務的市場龐大、潛力無窮,這會是我們準備迎戰的途徑之一。

各位可以研究其他相同主題的文章,繼續增加專門詞彙的蒐集。

專門字彙：職場老手篇

　　現在我們來看第二個情境，研究黛西如何準備 word partnerships，以便在面試中討論所應徵工作的相關議題。

　　黛西最近看到國際貨幣基金組織的求才廣告，覺得自己很適合這份工作。她把目標式 CV 和求職信寄給了國際貨幣基金組織，對方也邀請她去面試。黛西為了準備面試，先是回去重新閱讀求才廣告，將裡面的詞彙仔細研究了一番。以下便是國際貨幣基金組織的求才廣告。

Task 3.7

　　請閱讀這份求才廣告，找出 word partnerships 並畫上底線。

INTERNATIONAL MONEY FUND

For its headquarters in Washington, D.C., the International Money Fund (IMF) seeks

Qualified Accountants

The IMF desires accountants to participate in safeguards assessments of central banks. This policy evaluates member country central banks' control, accounting, reporting and auditing systems to ensure that financial resources, including those provided by the IMF, are adequately monitored and controlled.

The successful candidate is expected to prepare assessment reports, participate in missions to member countries, and contribute to the ongoing development of the conceptual safeguards assessment framework. Additional information concerning safeguards assessments can be found on the IMF's website under the heading "MF Finances."

Qualifications

▶ An advanced university degree in accounting, business administration, finance or economics, or equivalent, as well as professional certification in accounting (CPA/CA) are required.

▶ A minimum of three years of auditing experience, preferably with a large international accounting firm, and full knowledge of International Accounting Standards and International Standards on Auditing are required.

▶ Experience with central bank operations and knowledge of Mandarin or Cantonese is highly desirable.

國際貨幣基金會

國際貨幣基金會為華盛頓特區的總部誠徵．

合格會計師

國際貨幣基金會徵求會計師參與中央銀行防衛措施的評估。本政策評估會員國中央銀行的控管、會計、報告和審計系統，以確保金融資源受到適當監測和控制，包括國際貨幣基金會提供的資源。

應徵成功者將準備評估報告、隨團到會員國出差和參與持續建立中的概念性防衛措施評估架構。如欲得知關於防衛措施評估的其他資訊，請至國際貨幣基金會網站，參考以國際貨幣基金會財務為題的文章。

錄用資格

▶ 會計學、工商管理、財金或經濟學碩士學位或同等學歷，必須兼具專業會計師執照（執業會計師／特許會計師）。

▶ 三年以上審計經驗，在大型國際會計事務所工作者佳，對國際會計標準和國際審計標準有全面了解為必要條件。

▶ 具備中央銀行運作經驗，並且懂國語或廣東話者優先錄用。

Task **3.8**

現在請利用前面求才廣告的詞彙,填寫下面的 word partnerships 表。見範例。

V	Adj./Adv.	N
participate in	*safeguards*	*assessments*
participate in	—	
	accounting/reporting/auditing	
		resources
control		
		reports
	ongoing	

Task **3.7** 和 **3.8** ▶參考答案

如果會計不是你熟知的領域,或者覺得現在還不到向國際貨幣基金組織求職的階段,甚或是不太懂得這一份求才廣告中的詞彙,請不要擔心,目前的重點是介紹各位運用求才廣告,建立與所應徵公司和工作相關的 word partnerships。各位可以利用下表核對答案。

V	Adj./Adv.	N
participate in	safeguards	assessments
participate in	—	missions
evaluate	accounting/reporting/auditing	systems
monitor	financial	resources
control	financial	resources
prepare	assessment	reports
contribute to	ongoing	development

Task 3.9

　　黛西在面試中用了以下句子談論與工作相關的問題，請研究一下這些句子，並可利用 MP 3 練習聽和說。

> • I have quite a lot of experience in participating in safeguards assessments.
> • From my point of view, it's important to help organizations to monitor their financial resources.
> • In my last job I evaluated auditing systems for our clients, so I know how to do that.

Task 3.9 ▶參考答案

　　在下一單元將會為各位介紹如何造出這類句子，現在各位只需學習黛西如何在面試中運用那些從求才廣告中蒐集到的詞彙，顯現出她對工作相關議題的充分掌握，以及具有談論這些議題的口才和學識。

　　以下是黛西上面所用句子的中文翻譯，供各位參考：

> • 我參與防護措施評估的經驗豐富。
> • 在我看來，幫助機構監控財務資源是很重要的。
> • 在之前的工作中，我曾為客戶評估過審計系統，所以我知道怎麼做。

　　現在我們來看一看黛西如何準備 word partnerships，來以宏觀的角度談論國際貨幣基金組織的相關問題，以及談論國際貨幣基金組織在業界或領域中的一些最新發展。黛西上網用 Google 查詢 "IMF"，找到以下這篇討論國際貨幣基金組織在阿根廷遇到何種問題的文章。

Task 3.10

請閱讀這篇文章和譯文，然後回答下面問題，並可利用 MP3 練習聽力。

1. 根據文中的描述，阿根廷政府和國際貨幣基金組織的關係為何？
2. 阿根廷如何處理負債金額？
3. 阿根廷積欠國際貨幣基金組織多少錢？
4. 阿根廷的經濟計畫有哪些問題？

Argentina's massive debts and the IMF

BUENOS AIRES — Since he took over as Argentina's president last January, Eduardo Duhalde has been predicting both a speedy agreement with the IMF, and an economic recovery. Now there are signs that at least the first of these may happen quite soon. The Fund and the government "have made important progress in the past two weeks in an atmosphere of greater understanding of the Argentine political and economic situation," says Roberto Lavagna, the Argentine economy minister, though he cautions that not everything is yet confirmed.

Any deal with the IMF may owe more to the Fund's need to avoid the embarrassment of a new debt default than to Argentina's progress. While in default to its private creditors since December, Argentina has continued to service outstanding debts to international financial institutions — or some of them, at least. The IMF has been rolling over Argentina's repayments. However, it can only do this for twelve months. After that, a debtor in arrears risks eventual suspension from membership.

Argentina is due to repay US$10.8 billion to the IMF by December 2011, but has only US$9.4 billion in reserves. The government has suggested that from next month it will stop paying international institutions like the IMF and the World Bank. Given the size of its payments, that would not only damage the IMF's reputation, but even perhaps the World Bank's credit rating.

Many people in the Fund still have doubts about Argentina's economic program. The issues include whether privatized utilities are to be allowed to raise charges － frozen since January － and doubts over next year's national budget. In addition, the financial system is still in a disorganized state. Many bank deposits have been frozen since last December. But schemes to swap frozen deposits for government bonds have met some success. Officials have hinted that they may lift all remaining restrictions on current accounts next month. But this could provoke inflation.

阿根廷負債累累與國際貨幣基金組織

【布宜諾斯艾利斯報導】杜阿爾迪自從去年 1 月當上阿根廷總統以後，即預測會和國際貨幣基金組織迅速達成協議，據料經濟也將復甦，而現在已有種種跡象顯示，至少前者很快便會實現。經濟部長拉伐尼阿納表示，國際貨幣基金組織和政府「在過去兩個星期以來，已進一步達成重大協議，對方對阿根廷的政治和經濟狀況深表體諒」，不過他也謹慎地說一切尚未定案。

國際貨幣基金組織若達成任何協議，與其說是為了阿根廷的進步發展，事實上更大成分是為了避免再次發生債務逾期未繳帶來的尷尬。阿根廷自 12 月起便拖欠私人債權人債金，但仍繼續努力償還對國際金融組織的債務，或者至少已償還某些組織的債務：國際貨幣基金組織已多次為阿根廷延後償還期限。不過即使如此，國際貨幣基金組織也只能再給予阿根廷 12 個月的緩期，之後阿根廷便有可能被暫停會員資格。

阿根廷在 2011 年 12 月必須償還國際貨幣基金組織 108 億美元，卻只有 94 億美元的準備金。阿國政府建議從下個月起將不再支付國際機構，如國際貨幣基金組織和世界銀行。由於阿國政府的債務金額龐大，此法不僅會傷害國際貨幣基金組織的名聲，就連世界銀行的信用評等也要蒙塵。

國際貨幣基金組織會中有許多人對阿根廷的經濟計畫仍抱持懷疑態度，問題包括民營公用事業是否可以調漲費用（自 1 月起便凍結），以及對下一年度國家預算的懷疑。除此之外，阿國的金融體制仍然一片混亂，許多銀行存戶自去年 12 月便凍結了。不過以凍結存戶交換政府債券的方案收到了一些效果。有官員暗示下一個月可能移除所有其他對流動帳戶的限制，不過如此將可能導致通貨膨脹。

Task 3.10 ▶參考答案

1. 阿根廷最近選出了一名新總統，因此和國際貨幣基金組織會的關係已見好轉。新總統以新的經濟計畫爲重，以期改善阿國的經濟。

2. 阿根廷自 12 月起便無力償還對私人債權人的債務，但雖然對私人債權人違約，對國際機構如國際貨幣基金組織會卻沒有。

3. 阿根廷積欠國際貨幣基金組織會 108 億美元，但準備金卻只有 94 億美元。

4. 經濟計畫不無問題，包括公用事業費用凍結、明年的預算、金融體系一片混亂，以及受到通貨膨脹的威脅。

　　現在我們來看黛西如何利用這篇文章，建立用來談論所應徵公司、領域和業界的相關詞彙。

Task 3.11

請利用上面文章的詞彙填寫下面的 word partnerships 表格。見範例所示。

V	Adj./Adv.	N
predict	*speedy*	*agreement (with)*
predict		
	important	progress
	—	embarrassment
avoid		
		debts
roll over	—	
	—	membership
damage the IMF's	—	
	—	credit rating
	utility/bank/service	
	—	bank deposits
	—	restrictions
	—	inflation

Task 3.11 ▶參考答案

　　請利用下表核對答案。同樣地，若金融並非你所熟知的領域，或是不太懂得文章中的詞彙，不要擔心，這個習題主要是訓練各位從文章中挑出 word partnerships。

　　相信各位也注意到了，並非所有的 word partnerships 都有形容詞。

V	Adj./Adv.	N
predict	speedy	agreement (with)
predict	economic	recovery
make	important	progress
avoid	—	embarrassment
avoid	new	debt default
service	outstanding	debts
roll over	—	repayments
suspend sb. from	—	membership
damage the IMF's	—	reputation
damage	—	credit rating
raise	utility/bank/service	charges
freeze	—	bank deposits
lift	—	restrictions
provoke	—	inflation

Task 3.12

　　請研究下面例句，黛西在面試時使用這些句子討論國際貨幣基金組織所面對的議題，以及業界中的相關議題。

- I'd say that rolling over repayments is not a bad thing, but there's always the danger that doing so will damage the reputation of the IMF.
- I'm convinced that debtor countries need to lift restrictions on current accounts.
- In my opinion, this will not provoke inflation because interest rates are still quite high on domestic loans.

Task　3.12　▶參考答案

　　請注意黛西在面試中如何運用從文章中蒐集到的詞彙，展現出她對公司和業界相關議題的充分了解，以及談論這些議題的口才。在下一單元中將會為各位介紹如何造出這類句子。

　　以下是黛西前面所用句子的中文翻譯，供各位參考：

> • 我不認為延後償還期限是一件壞事，但這個做法一定會有破壞國際貿易基金會形象之虞。
> • 我深深覺得債務國應該取消對經常性帳戶的限制。
> • 我不認為這個做法會引起通貨膨脹，因為國內貸款利率仍居高不下。

　　各位可以研究其他相同主題的文章，持續增加這類專門詞彙。

　　現在我們來了解一下凱文和黛西是如何建立詞彙的。首先，在面試之前，他們倆人都花了些時間在家自己用 MP3 播放器練習談論這些議題，並錄下自己的話。其次，當他們遇到不懂的英文詞彙，或者有些想法只會用中文但不會用英文表達時，他們會用中文記錄下來，然後繼續講下去。最後，等到練習完畢，他們便會翻閱字典把那些中文詞彙翻譯成英文，然後再用英文說出自己的看法，如此同步進行面試準備和建立詞彙庫。

Task　3.13

　　練習談論關於自己領域或行業的議題。如果遇到不知道如何運用的英文詞彙，先用中文寫在下表中，等練習完畢，再翻閱字典將這些中文詞彙翻譯成英文。

Chinese	English

 面試問題的應答演練

好，我們已經研究過準備詞彙的方法，懂得如何談論工作相關的議題，以及業界或公司所面對的議題了。此外還學會將那些不會用英文表達的中文詞彙記下來，以擴增詞彙庫。現在要開始研究面試時可能會問到的問題了。

Task 3.14

請看以下這些面試可能會問到的 101 個問題，勾出符合自己工作環境的問題。

1. Are you a leader?	
2. Are you a loner?	
3. Are you accepted into a team quickly?	
4. Are you aggressive?	
5. Are you competitive?	
6. Are you considering any other positions at the moment?	
7. Are you prepared to relocate?	
8. Are you self-motivated, or do you need other people around to stimulate you?	
9. Are you willing to travel abroad?	
10. Can you act on your own initiative?	
11. Can you motivate other people?	
12. Did you increase profits or sales in your last job?	
13. Did you reduce costs at your last company? How did you do this?	
14. Did your previous company live up to your expectations?	
15. Do you consider yourself successful? Why?	
16. Do you feel you are ready to take on a lot of responsibility?	
17. Do you feel you are ready to take on more responsibility?	
18. Do you feel you made good progress in your last job?	
19. Do you prefer working in a small, medium or large company? Why?	

20. Do you think your college studies have prepared you for the real world of work?	
21. Do you work well under pressure?	
22. Do you work well with other people?	
23. Don't you think you are over-qualified for this position?	
24. Don't you think you are too old for this job?	
25. Don't you think you are too young for this job?	
26. Explain the organizational structure of your last company and how you fitted into it.	
27. Have you ever been fired?	
28. How ambitious are you?	
29. How could you improve yourself?	
30. How did you get along with your previous manager or supervisor, co-workers and subordinates?	
31. How do you chair a meeting?	
32. How do you deal with criticism?	
33. How do you feel about working for someone of the opposite sex?	
34. How do you feel about working for someone older than yourself?	
35. How do you feel about working for someone younger than you?	
36. How do you feel about working long hours of overtime with no pay?	
37. How do you think working is going to be different from being a student?	
38. How do you think working life will be different from student life?	
39. How good are you at managing money?	
40. How good are you at managing people?	
41. How good are you at managing stress?	
42. How good are you at managing your time?	
43. How long do you think it would be before you were making a significant contribution to our team/company?	
44. How long do you think you will stay in this job?	
45. How long have you been between jobs?	

46. How long have you been looking for a job?	
47. How many hours are you prepared to work?	
48. How much does your last job resemble the one you are applying for? What are the differences?	
49. How often are you off sick?	
50. How would other people describe you?	
51. How would you describe yourself?	
52. In your previous job, what did you do on a day-to-day basis?	
53. Tell me about what you did in your previous job.	
54. Tell me something about your interests and hobbies.	
55. What activities did you do in college that you think have prepared you for working in a company?	
56. What annoyed you about your last job?	
57. What are the differences between the job you are applying for and the last job you had?	
58. What are you doing at the moment?	
59. What are you looking for in a new job?	
60. What are your main job duties in your current job?	
61. What are you most proud of in your career?	
62. What are you working on at the moment?	
63. What are your career aims?	
64. What can the new company offer that your previous company cannot?	
65. What can you contribute?	
66. What did you learn in college?	
67. What did you learn in your last job?	
68. What did you think of your manager or supervisor?	
69. What do you dislike about the job you have applied for?	
70. What do you dislike doing? Why?	
71. What do you know about (sth. connected to the company, its industry, or markets)?	

72. What do you know about this company?	
73. What do you think of (a current event happening in the industry)?	
74. What do you think of (an ethical issue facing the industry)?	
75. What do you think of your last company?	
76. What have you been doing in the time between your last job and now?	
77. What interests you about our company/industry/service/product?	
78. What level of salary are you looking for now?	
79. What makes a good manager?	
80. What management style gets the best results out of you?	
81. What motivates you?	
82. What pleased you about your last job?	
83. What qualities do you think are required for this job?	
84. What sort of manager are you?	
85. What will your referees not say about you?	
86. What will your referees say about you?	
87. What would you like to avoid in your next job?	
88. What would your ideal job be?	
89. What's the best job you've ever had and why?	
90. What's the best way to chair a meeting?	
91. What's the worst job you've ever had and why?	
92. What's your career plan?	
93. Why are you changing careers?	
94. Why are you leaving your current company now?	
95. Why are you leaving your current job?	
96. Why did you choose a career in (your field)?	
97. Why did you join your previous company?	
98. Why do you want this job?	
99. Why do you want to work for this company?	
100. Why should we employ you?	
101. Would you compete for my job?	

Task 3.14 ▶參考答案

　　若各位對這 101 個問題有不瞭解的地方，可參閱本單元最後所附的句子中譯。

　　我一定不會知道哪一些問題符合各位的工作環境，但是我確信只要各位仔細研究這些問題，一定看得出其中有些問題適用於社會新鮮人，有些則適合工作資歷較深、年紀較長的求職者。

　　為面試做好萬全準備是極其重要的。如果面試官問你一個艱深的問題，絕對不可以啞口無言。要是你不知道如何回答，或者看起來好像從沒想過問題所涉及的議題，這樣是無法留給對方好印象的。

Task 3.15

　　請研究符合各位工作環境的問題，著手準備該如何回應這些問題。並可利用 MP3 播放器錄下答案，同時增補詞彙庫，將需要用到的詞彙記錄下來。

Task 3.15 ▶參考答案

　　在此各位應該著重於回答的內容和詞彙，也就是回答時會用到的 word partnerships 即可。在下一單元中將會學習口說技巧的部分，也會介紹各位一些 set-phrases，幫助各位回答得更加精準和自然。

　　前面的問題有些可能看起來很奇怪，或許是各位從來都沒想到過的，但千萬不要因而省略不看。記住，準備面試是不怕一萬只怕萬一，絕對不可掉以輕心。

　　好了，我們接下來要學習在面試時可以用上的一些關鍵詞，不過在此之前先來鞏固之前學到的詞彙準備技巧。

Task 3.16

請用號碼按照順序將下面準備步驟標示出來。請參見標示出的第一個步驟。

Google an article about the company you are going to be interviewed by.	
Practice putting them into sentences using some of the MWIs from unit 4.	
Practice the pronunciation.	
Practice the pronunciation.	
Read the article and understand the content.	
Read the job advertisement carefully.	1
Repeat with more articles, building a bank of word partnerships.	
Underline all the word partnerships in the article. Put them into a table.	
Underline all the word partnerships in the job advertisement. Put them into a table.	

Task 3.16 ▶參考答案　　　　　　　　　　　　　　　　　29

詞彙準備步驟的正確順序如下。

① Read the job advertisement carefully.
② Underline all the word partnerships in the job advertisement. Put them into a table.
③ Practice the pronunciation.
④ Google an article about the company you are going to be interviewed by.
⑤ Read the article and understand the content.
⑥ Underline all the word partnerships in the article. Put them into a table.
⑦ Practice the pronunciation.
⑧ Repeat with more articles, building a bank of word partnerships.
⑨ Practice putting them into sentences using some of the MWIs from unit 4.

好，我們繼續往下學習面試中可以用上的關鍵詞彙吧。

求職達人基本功：面試關鍵字

Task 3.17

請研究下面和 experience 連用的 word partnerships 以及下方的例句。並請試著在空白欄寫上自己的造句。可利用 MP3 練習倒句的聽和說。

V	Adj.		N
have	first-hand	useful	
apply	hands-on	wide	
acquire	invaluable	a wealth of	
gain	extensive	early	experience
provide	practical	fascinating	
	previous	learning	
	valuable	testing	

- I'm looking for a job where I can **apply** my **extensive experience** in simultaneous translation.
- I'd like to **gain** some more **hands-on experience**.
- I **have a wealth of experience** in crisis management.
- In my last job I **gained** a lot of **practical experience** with client relations.
- _____
- _____

Task 3.17 ▶參考答案

在此提供上面例句的中譯給各位參考：

- 我想找到一份同步翻譯的工作，因為我累積了很多這方面的經驗。
- 我希望得到更多的實務經驗。
- 我的危機管理經驗很豐富。
- 在之前的工作中，我得到許多客戶關係方面的實際經驗。

Task **3.18**

　請研究下面和 skills 連用的 word partnerships 以及下方的例句。並請試著在空白欄寫上自己的造句。記得聽例句的 MP3 音調和發音喔。

V	Adj.		N
learn	supervisory	necessary	
develop	management	old	
apply	interpersonal	planning	
acquire	problem solving	communication	
practice	analytical	existing	skills
bring	people	professional	
offer	transferable	technical	
work on	new	a set of	
improve	leadership	organizational	

- I'm keen to **develop** better **communication skills**.
- I wanted to **practice** my **analytical skills** more.
- I think I can **bring** good **interpersonal skills** to the job.
- I've been **working on** my **problem solving skills**, and I'm eager to try them out in a new environment.
- _____
- _____
- _____

Task **3.18** ▶參考答案

　在此提供上面例句的中譯給各位參考：

- 我對建立更好的溝通技巧有高度興趣。
- 我對加強練習分析技巧有高度興趣。
- 我覺得我可以為這份工作貢獻良好的人際關係技巧。
- 我一直在加強解決問題的技巧，熱切希望在新環境中嘗試這些技巧。

Task 3.19

請研究下面和 prospects 連用的 word partnerships 以及下方的例句。並請試著在空白欄寫上自己的造句。同樣地，可善加利用 MP3 練習聽和說。

V	Adj.	N
have	bright	
offer	challenging	
provide	excellent	
open up	exciting	prospects (for)
see	fascinating	
weigh up	promising	
	stimulating	

- My previous job didn't provide enough challenging prospects for me.
- I'm looking for something with brighter prospects.
- I'm hoping that this job will open up some more interesting prospects for me.
- I saw the job listing and I thought I could see some exciting prospects here.
- _____
- _____
- _____

Task 3.19 ▶參考答案

在此提供上面例句的中譯給各位參考：

- 我之前的工作給我的挑戰不夠。
- 我在尋找比較有展望的工作。
- 我希望這份工作能為我開展更有意思的前景。
- 我看到工作一覽表，覺得似乎會有令人期待的展望。

Task 3.20

　　請研究下面和 challenge 連用的 word partnerships 以及下方的例句。並請試著在空白欄寫上自己的造句。請聽 MP3 的例句示範。

V	Adj.	N
look for	more of	
need	bigger	
offer	big	challenge (of/for)
respond to	exciting	
take up	real	
be enough of	tough	

- I'm looking for more of a challenge.
- My previous company wasn't able to respond to the challenge of globalization.
- I'm eager to take up a bigger challenge.
- I don't think my previous job was enough of a real challenge for me.
- _____
- _____
- _____

Task 3.20 ▶參考答案

　　在此提供上面例句的中譯給各位參考：

- 我希望挑戰性比較高。
- 我之前的公司無法因應全球化的挑戰。
- 我急於接受更大的挑戰。
- 我覺得之前的工作挑戰性不足。

　　好，在往下學習下一個單元之前，請先回到本單元前面的學習目標的清單，把達成的目標逐項打勾，確認每一項都切實學會了再繼續看下一個單元。

面試時可能會問到的 101 個問題中譯：

1. 你有領導能力嗎？

2. 你孤僻嗎？

3. 你是否能很快融入團隊？

4. 你有侵略性嗎？

5. 你喜歡競爭嗎？

6. 你目前有沒有考慮任何其他職位？

7. 你願意被派往他處工作嗎？

8. 你是否能夠自我激勵，還是需要靠身邊其他人激勵你？

9. 你願意出國出差嗎？

10. 你會自動自發嗎？

11. 你能不能激勵他人？

12. 你在之前的工作中有沒有為公司提高收入或業績？

13. 你有沒有為之前的公司減少成本？你是怎麼辦到的？

14. 你之前的公司有沒有符合你的期望？

15. 你認為自己成功嗎？

16. 你覺得自己有沒有做好準備，肩負起很多責任？

17. 你覺得自己有沒有做好準備，肩負起更多責任？

18. 你覺得自己在之前的工作中有沒有進步很多？

19. 你比較喜歡在小型、中型還是大型的公司上班？

20. 你覺得在大學念的書對你面對職場的真實世界有沒有幫助？

21. 你在壓力大的環境下能不能照樣工作？

22. 你能不能和別人共事？

23. 你不覺得自己資歷太高，不適合這個職位嗎？

24. 你不覺得自己年紀太大，不適合這份工作嗎？

25. 你不覺得自己年紀太小，不適合這份工作嗎？

26. 請說說看你之前公司的組織架構，以及你部門在這架構中的位置。

27. 你有沒有被解僱過？

28. 你的企圖心有多大？

29. 你可以如何改進自己？

30. 你和之前的經理／主管、同事和下屬相處得如何？

31. 你都如何主持會議？

32. 你如何面對批評？

33. 你對在異性主管之下工作有何看法？

34. 你對在年齡比自己大的主管之下工作有何看法？

35. 你對在年齡比自己小的主管之下工作有何看法？

36. 你對長時間加班但沒有加班費有何看法？

37. 你覺得上班和當學生會有什麼不同？

38. 你覺得上班族的生活和學生生活會有什麼不同？

39. 你善不善於處理金錢？

40. 你善不善於管理人？

41. 你善不善於管理壓力？

42. 你善不善於管理時間？

43. 你覺得你在多久之後會開始對我們的團隊／公司有大貢獻？

44. 你覺得這份工作你會做多久？

45. 你待業多久了？

46. 你找工作找多久了？

47. 你能夠上幾小時的班？

48. 你之前的工作和現在應徵的工作有哪些相似之處？有哪些不同之處？

49. 你多常請病假？

50. 別人會如何描述你？

51. 你會如何描述你自己？

52. 在之前的工作中你的日常職務為何？

53. 請說說看你在之前的工作做了哪些事情。

54. 請談一談你的興趣和嗜好。

55. 你覺得在大學從事過哪些活動，是對日後在公司上班有幫助的？

56. 你之前的工作有什麼地方曾讓你感到很困擾？

57. 你應徵的工作和你之前的工作有何不同之處？

58. 你目前在做什麼？

59. 你希望找什麼樣的新工作？

60. 你目前工作的主要職責有哪些？

61. 你對自己事業中感到最自豪的事情是什麼？

62. 你目前在從事什麼事情？

63. 你的事業目標爲何？

64. 有什麼東西是我們（新公司）能夠提供，而你之前公司無法提供給你的？

65. 你能帶來什麼樣的貢獻？

66. 你在大學學到了什麼？

67. 你從之前的工作學到了什麼？

68. 你對你的經理／主管有何看法？

69. 你對應徵的工作有何不滿意之處？

70. 你不喜歡做什麼事？

71. 你對（與公司、業界或市場有關的事情）有何了解？

72. 你對本公司有何了解？

73. 你對（……業界中發生的最新事件）有何看法？

74. 你對（……業界面臨的倫理議題）有何看法？

75. 你對之前的公司有何看法？

76. 從離開之前的工作到現在，你都在做什麼事情？

77. 你對我們公司／產業／服務／產品有何興趣？

78. 你現在希望有多少薪資？

79. 怎麼樣才能成爲好的經理？

80. 什麼樣的管理風格最能讓你發揮潛力？

81. 你的動力來源爲何？

82. 你對之前的工作有何滿意之處？

83. 你覺得做這份工作應該有哪些人格特質？

84. 你是什麼樣的經理？

85. 你有哪些事是推薦人不會說的？

86. 你的推薦人會如何形容你？

87. 你希望在之後的工作中避免哪些事情？

88. 你的理想工作爲何？

89. 你至今做過最棒的工作為何？為什麼？

90. 會議應該如何主持最好？

91. 你至今做過最差的工作為何？為什麼？

92. 你的職業規劃為何？

93. 你為什麼要轉換職業跑道？

94. 為什麼你現在想離開目前的公司？

95. 為什麼你要離開目前的工作？

96. 為什麼你選擇從事……？

97. 你為什麼進入之前的公司？

98. 為什麼你希望得到這份工作？

99. 你為什麼希望在本公司工作？

100. 我們為什麼要僱用你？

101. 你會爭取我現在這個職位嗎？

Unit （4）

實戰面試
During the Interview

引言與學習目標

　　面試官知道英文並非各位的母語，所以不會期望各位說出一口流利的標準英文，事實上，很可能連面試官自己都不是以英文為母語呢。這樣看來其實無須過度擔心英文程度不夠好的事，因為只要按照上一單元教過的訣竅準備面試，儲備的詞彙應該足以應付面試，也知道可能會被問到哪些問題。只是話雖如此，以流暢的英文留給對方深刻的印象還是必要的，所以千萬不要掉以輕心。在面試的時候不用擔心文法正不正確，重點是向對方流暢地傳達想法。

　　在本單元中我們要學習一些 set-phrases，用於回答面試中的問題，也可以用來向對方提出自己的問題。

　　本單元的學習結束之時，各位應該達成的學習目標如下：

- ❏ 知道面試中會遇到什麼樣的狀況。
- ❏ 學到一些 set-phrases，可謙虛地談論自己並表達看法。
- ❏ 學到一些訣竅和 set-phrases，用於談論自己的成就和失敗經驗。
- ❏ 學到一些訣竅和 set-phrases，用於描述自己目前和過去的工作內容。
- ❏ 學到一些訣竅和 set-phrases，用於談論自己對未來事業的生涯規畫。
- ❏ 學到一些訣竅和 set-phrases，用於回應負面的問題。
- ❏ 學到一些訣竅和 set-phrases，可和面試官自然的互動和組織回答內容。
- ❏ 學到一些訣竅和 set-phrases，用於向面試官提出問題。
- ❏ 知道基本的標準發音和做過許多發音練習。
- ❏ 做過許多聽力練習。
- ❏ 做過許多回答問題的練習。

求職面試的流程

現在我們就從求職面試的架構開始學起，讓你對面試的流程有一點概念。

Task 4.1

請按照順序將以下的面試步驟填寫在流程圖中。

- Conclusion
- Greetings and small talk
- Interviewer asks general questions about you and your experience
- Interviewer asks more specific questions about how you would handle certain situations
- You ask questions about the company and job

Task 4.1 ▶參考答案

請根據下面的面試流程圖檢查答案，然後閱讀解析。

1	2	3	4	5
Greetings and small talk	Interviewer asks general questions about you and your experience	Interviewer asks more specific questions about how you would handle certain situations	You ask questions about the company and job	Conclusion

面試流程解析

▶ 這是一個很基本的面試流程。通常在面試中，雙方會在自我介紹之後開聊一下。面試官會想讓你放輕鬆，問你面試地點會不會難找或者要不要喝飲料，或者也可能聊一下天氣等話題。這時可以盡量放輕鬆，調整到舒服的坐姿，然後優雅地交腿並將雙手交疊放在腿上。

▶ 第二和第三階段是面試的主體，這時面試官很可能會問到上一單元中各位已經學過的問題。仔細地聽，然後完整而自然地回答即可，並舉出大量的實例。聽不懂問題時不要覺得不好意思，可以請面試官將問題重複一遍。

▶ 進入面試的第四階段時，面試官會詢問你是否有想問的問題。這時你一定要開口提問，如果沒問，面試官覺得你好像興趣缺缺，不然就是太害羞或對公司、業界面對的議題一無所知。或許你在事前做了很多準備功夫，對公司和工作本身已經瞭若指掌，以致沒有什麼問題想問，但即便如此還是一定得問個問題。此外，面試官也會以你所提問題的水準，來當作選用人才的判斷依據，因此一定要詢問對方有關市場狀況、公司目前面對的問題和挑戰等，和面試官短暫互動，如此可向對方表現出自己豐富的知識，以及對公司和業界的背景已有所了解。同時，你也有機會展現自己從背景研究當中學到的知識，炫耀一下面試前所準備的詞彙。

▶ 當面試官結束面試時，切記要向對方表示感謝抽空面試你，禮貌道別後才行離開。在離開辦公大樓之前都得保持冷靜，因為直到離開大樓，面試才算正式結束。

　　現在我們來研究一下面試第二、三階段會用到的一些語彙。先從表達看法（giving opinion）的語彙切入，然後進入謙虛地談論自己（talking modestly about yourself）的語彙，這兩項表達對學習英文的中文人士來說特別困難，因為其中存有文化差異的問題。

求職達人基本功：發音

在繼續往下學習之前，我們要先利用 MP3 光碟練習一些 set-phrases 的發音。在面試時發音絕對要力求清楚。就算你的英文很好，不僅詞彙豐富而且文法高明，但是若是口音太重，面試官對你的英文還是會有負面觀感。所以，即使你的文法並不夠好，詞彙也不足，但是發音準確又漂亮，面試官對你的英文仍然會留下深刻的印象。

要想達到發音清楚，有兩個技巧必須勤加練習，那就是：連音和語調。以下將分別介紹這兩項技巧的練習要訣。

連音

連珠帶砲似地講英文時，字詞自然而然便會串聯在一塊兒，以至於兩個字聽起來就像是一個字。所以，只要掌握連音技巧，你的英文聽起來必定會更加流暢，同樣地，了解連音的技巧之後也能幫助你聽懂對方的問題。

用 MP3 光碟練習發音的時候，別忘了要以講者為榜樣，盡量跟上他說話的速度。仔細聽講者串聯字詞的方法。

語調

所謂語調是指說話時聲音的抑揚頓挫。許多中文人士的英文聽起來平平板板，這是中文不要求語調使然，導致講英文時語調沒有起伏。然而講英文時語調平板會給人乏味、不友善甚至有一點敵意的感覺，所以最好不要套用中文的方式在英文口說上。

用 MP3 光碟練習發音的時候，別忘了要以講者為榜樣，盡量模仿他說話的語調，甚至稍為誇張一點都無妨。仔細聽講者講到什麼詞會提高語調，講到什麼詞又會降低語調。

發表謙遜的看法和談論自己

別忘了，西方人會期望你能發表自己的看法。如果你的面試官是西方人，那麼對方一定會詢問你對公司本身、公司業務和所應徵的工作等方面的看法。不要感到害羞，直接將想法說出來吧。如果各位有按照上一單元中介紹的秘訣做好準備，各位的詞彙應該就足以用來表達自己的看法了。

另一個問題是，中國文化講求謙遜，不應該炫耀個人成就。不過在求職面試時要是太過謙遜，不好意思談及個人成就，面試官如何知道各位到底優不優秀呢？！最好的辦法就是做得恰到好處，既能顧及謙虛的禮貌，又能讓面試官知道各位在事業上的成就。我們接下來要學習的 set-phrases 便可以幫助各位取得這個平衡。

Task 4.2

請將以下這些 chunks 和 set-phrases 加以分類，寫在後表所屬的欄位中。

As far as I can make out, ...	I think ...
As I see it, ...	I'd say that ...
From my point of view, ...	I'm committed to n.p./Ving ...
I always aim for n.p.	I'm convinced that ...
I always aim to V ...	I'm told that I'm ...
I always give my all to n.p.	I've been told that I'm ...
I always go for n.p.	In my experience, ...
I always insist on n.p.	In my opinion, ...
I always try to V ...	In my view, ...
I believe ...	It seems to me that ...
I firmly believe ...	It's often said of me that I'm ...
I personally think ...	My own view is that ...
I reckon ...	My position is that ...
I suspect that ...	My view is that ...
I think I'm effective at n.p./Ving ...	People say that I'm ...
I think I'm good at n.p./Ving ...	There's no doubt in my mind that ...
I think I'm quite adj.	To my mind, ...
I think my strengths are ...	To my way of thinking, ...

Talking modestly about yourself

Giving your opinion

Task **4.2** ▶參考答案

　　請利用下面的必備語庫核對答案。

求職必備語庫 **4.1** ▶聽力 4.1

Talking modestly about yourself

I always aim for n.p.	I think I'm quite adj.
I always aim to V ...	I think my strengths are ...
I always give my all to n.p.	I'm committed to n.p./Ving ...
I always go for n.p.	I'm told that I'm ...
I always insist on n.p.	I've been told that I'm ...
I always try to V ...	It's often said of me that I'm ...
I think I'm effective at n.p./Ving ...	People say that I'm ...
I think I'm good at n.p./Ving ...	

Giving your opinion

As far as I can make out, ...	In my experience, ...
As I see it, ...	In my opinion, ...
From my point of view, ...	In my view, ...
I believe ...	It seems to me that ...
I firmly believe ...	My own view is that ...
I personally think ...	My position is that ...
I reckon ...	My view is that ...
I suspect that ...	There's no doubt in my mind that ...
I think ...	To my mind, ...
I'd say that ...	To my way of thinking, ...
I'm convinced that ...	

　　以上這些 set-phrases 可用來談論自己並同時保持低調，雖然各位可能看不出來，覺得還是有誇耀的感覺存在！事實上，這些 set-phrases 確實是滿低調的，面試官聽到各位用這些 set-phrases 表達看法絕對會很滿意。

Task 4.3

　　請練習必備語庫 4.1 中的 set-phrases，可利用 MP3 中的聽力 4.1 輔助練習。

Task 4.4

　　請看以下這些問題，選出最符合自己狀況的問題，然後運用剛學到的 set-phrases 來練習回答。

Are you a leader?	
Are you a loner?	
Are you accepted into a team quickly?	
Are you aggressive?	
Are you competitive? How so?	
Are you considering any other positions at the moment?	
Are you self-motivated, or do you need other people around to stimulate you?	

Can you act on your own initiative?	
Can you motivate other people?	
Do you think your college studies have prepared you for the real world of work?	
Don't you think you are over-qualified for this position? Why or why not?	
Don't you think you are too old for this job?	
Don't you think you are too young for this job?	
How ambitious are you?	
How could you improve yourself?	
How do you chair a meeting?	
How do you deal with criticism?	
How do you feel about working for someone of the opposite sex?	
How do you feel about working for someone older than yourself?	
How do you feel about working for someone younger than you?	
How do you think working is going to be different from being a student?	
How do you think working life will be different from student life?	
How long do you think it would be before you were making a significant contribution to our team/company?	
How would other people describe you?	
How would you describe yourself?	
What can you contribute?	
What did you think of your previous manager/supervisor?	
What do you know about (something connected to the company, its industry, or markets)?	
What do you know about this company?	
What do you think of (a current event happening in the industry)?	
What do you think of (an ethical issue facing the industry)?	
What interests you about our company/industry/service/product?	
What makes a good manager?	
What management style gets the best results out of you?	
What motivates you?	
What qualities do you think are required for this job?	
What sort of manager are you?	
What will your referees not say about you?	
What will your referees say about you?	
What's the best way to chair a meeting?	
Why do you want this job?	
Why do you want to work for this company?	
Why should we employ you?	

我們現在要來看看幾個範例，學習凱文和黛西利用必備語庫 4.1 中的 set-phrases 來回答問題的方法。我們先從凱文的回答開始看起。

Task 4.5 ▶聽力 4.2

請閱讀以下範例，研究凱文回答問題的方法，然後從他的回答中找出先前學到的 set-phrases，並畫上底線。注意這些 set-phrases 的用法，並利用聽力 4.2 培養臨場感。

> Interviewer: How would you describe yourself?

> Kevin: Well, let me see. I think I'm quite ambitious. I want to succeed and have a good career. I always aim to do my best in a situation–you know? What I mean is, I always try to look for the best way to do something. I think I'm good at spotting problems and finding ways to fix them.

> Interviewer: What do you think of the future of the luxury car market in China?

> Kevin: Well, it seems to me that it's a growth market, especially in after-sales service. I'd say that as China liberalizes, and as the people get richer, there are going to be more opportunities in this market. What's more, I firmly believe it's the best market to be in right now.

Task 4.5 ▶參考答案

請利用以下凱文回答的中文翻譯來檢核自己的理解力吧。

面試官：你會如何描述自己？

凱　文：嗯，我想一想。我覺得自己滿有企圖心的，我希望成功和事業有成。我遇到事情總會全力以赴，你知道的。我的意思是說，我每次都會努力尋找做事的最佳方式。我想我對發現問題，然後找到方法解決問題很在行。

面試官：你覺得中國的豪華汽車市場前景如何？

凱　文：嗯，我看這個市場成長空間很大，尤其是售後服務這塊市場。我覺得當中國越來越開放、大家越來越富裕，這個市場一定會出現更多的機會。除此之外，我堅信現在進佔這塊市場最好。

Task　4.6 ▶ 聽力 4.3　　　　　　　　　　　　　　　　　　

現在請閱讀以下範例，研究黛西回答問題的方法，然後從她的回答中找出先前學到的 set-phrases，並畫上底線。注意這些 set-phrases 的用法，並利用聽力 4.3 培養臨場感。

Interviewer:	How would you describe yourself?

Daisy:	Well, in my personal life, I'm quite easygoing, but at work, I always go for perfection. I mean, the numbers have always got to be correct, haven't they, so I always insist on 100 percent accuracy and care. I've been told that I'm a perfectionist, you know, people say that I'm quite strict about getting the numbers correct.

Interviewer:	What do you think of countries who default on their loans to the IMF?

Daisy:	Hmm. That's a difficult one. Obviously, defaulted loans cost the IMF and hurt the organization badly—you know, damage its creditability. On the other hand, I'm convinced that most countries try hard not to default

on their loans because then it damages their creditability too. Not only that, but also, I reckon that economic circumstances change so quickly that sometimes it's impossible to pay back a loan within the timeframe. To my way of thinking, a balance needs to be reached between the needs of the IMF, and the needs of the borrowers. Let me put it this way: I believe that everything can always be negotiated, and it's up to the IMF and borrowers to negotiate a settlement that suits both parties.

Task 4.6 ▶參考答案

請利用以下黛西回答的中文翻譯來檢核自己的理解力吧。

面試官：你會如何描述自己？

黛　西：哦，私底下我滿隨和的，但在工作時我一定追求完美。我的意思是說，沒有一個數字可以出錯，是不是？所以我總是堅持 100% 的準確和謹慎。有人說我是完美主義者，是這樣的，他們說我對數字的正確性要求很高。

面試官：有些國家未能將貸款債務歸還給國際貨幣基金會，你對這些國家的看法為何？

黛　西：嗯，這個問題很複雜。顯然對方未能償還債務，對國際貨幣基金會造成金錢上的損失，組織也會受到嚴重傷害，我是指信譽受損。但反過來說，我相信大部分的國家都會努力不拖欠債務，因為他們的信譽也是會受損。不僅如此，我覺得經濟狀況變化快速，有時不大可能在規定時間內清償款項。我的看法是，國際貨幣基金會和貸款國的需求必須從中尋找到一個平衡點。這樣說吧，我認為沒有事情是不能商量的，國際貨幣基金會和貸款國應該協商，找到雙方都滿意的解決方法。

既然各位已經看過以上這些範例，現在應該知道如何回答這些問題了吧？那就請以自己的角度練習回答這些問題。請不斷練習，直到有信心能夠應答如流爲止，然後再繼續做下面的練習。

Task **4.7** ▶ 聽力 4.4

請聽聽力 4.4 中的問題，這些問題和 Task 4.4 的問題一致，只是順序不同。請在聽完每個問題之後先按暫停，試著自己回答，並錄下答案，以供播聽改進。

Task **4.7** ▶ 參考答案

▷ MP3 中的問題和 Task 4.4 的順序不同，這是爲了提高各位在練習時的難度！記住，在面試時一定要隨時做好準備，迎戰出其不意的問題。

▷ 特別注意自己說 set-phrases 的方式。語調有明顯的抑揚頓挫嗎？聽起來是否夠流利？尚能如何改進自己的應答？

好了，現在我們要繼續往下學習其他技巧，談論過去工作上的成就和失敗經驗。

 談論成就和失敗經驗

面試官會很重視你對成就和失敗經驗的說明。別忘了，對方在意的不僅僅是你的成就和失敗經驗，還包括你如何描述這些事情，因為藉由觀察你回答這個問題的恰當與否，面試官能從中對你做出很大的判斷。

如果談論自己的成就時過於高傲，你會留下惡劣的印象，反過來說，你也應該對曾經經歷的失敗據實以告，但是之後務必要強調從中學到的教訓，才能為自己加分。

我們來學習一些 set-phrases，討論經歷過的成就和失敗。

Task 4.8

請將以下這些 set-phrases 加以分類，寫在下頁所屬的欄位中。

However, it was a positive learning experience for me.	I could have done better at Ving ...
I didn't manage to V ...	I successfully managed to V ...
I had some success at Ving ...	I was able to V...
I managed to V ...	I could have done better to V ...
I succeeded in Ving ...	I was successful in Ving ...
However, I learned a lot about n.p.	Unfortunately, I wasn't able to V ...
One of the things I'm most proud of is the way that + clause.	One of the things I'm most proud of is n.p.
I didn't really know n.p.	One of my least successful experiences was n.p.
What I should have done was + clause.	One of my least successful experiences was when + clause.

Talking about successes

Talking about failures

Task 4.8 ▶參考答案

　　請利用下面的必備語庫核對答案，然後閱讀語庫解析。

求職必備語庫 **4.2** ▶聽力 4.5

Talking about successes
I had some success at Ving ...
I managed to V ...
I succeeded in Ving ...
One of the things I'm most proud of is n.p.
I successfully managed to V ...
I was able to V ...
I was successful in Ving ...
One of the things I'm most proud of is the way that + clause.

Talking about failures

However, I learned a lot about n.p.

However, it was a positive learning experience for me.

One of my least successful experiences was n.p.

I didn't really know n.p.

I could have done better at Ving ...

I could have done better to V ...

I didn't manage to V ...

Unfortunately, I wasn't able to V ...

One of my least successful experiences was when + clause.

What I should have done was + clause.

語庫解析

▶ I managed to V 是用來描述成就，而 I managed n.p. 卻是用來描述職務內容。在本單元後面將會為各位介紹談論職務內容的用語。

▶ 描述完經歷過的失敗，用 However, I learned a lot about n.p. 和 However, it was a positive learning experience for me 來做結尾。各位應該誠實地說明曾經犯下的錯誤。每個人都有過失敗的經驗，要是說自己從來沒有失敗過，面試官是不會相信你的。不過，最後一定要談到從中學到的教訓，讓整個事情聽起來是正面的，這樣面試官就會知道你了解自己的缺點，而且有心改進。

▶ 說明失敗的時候要說 One of my least successful experiences ...，而不要說 One of my worst experiences was ...，聽起來才會比較正面。

Task 4.9

請聽聽力 4.5，練習必備語庫 4.2 中 set-phrases 的發音。

Task 4.10

請利用剛剛學到的 set-phrases 練習回答以下問題。

❏ Tell me about one of your successes.
❏ Tell me about your biggest failure.

回答問題的時候一定要注意「時態」。既然是談論過去的經驗就務必要用過去簡單式。我們來看一看凱文和黛西如何運用 set-phrases 回答問題，以及他們所使用的時態。先以凱文的回答當範例，從他所運用的 set-phrases 開始學起。

Task 4.11 ▶聽力 4.6

請閱讀以下凱文對過去成就的說明，從中找出先前學過的 set-phrases，並畫上底線，然後再找出所有的動詞並畫上底線，注意凱文所用的時態。請利用聽力 4.6 培養臨場感。

Interviewer: Tell me about one of your successes.

Kevin: Well, let me think now. One of the things I'm most proud of was the way I managed to bring in two big customers to Campho when I worked there. I knew of this big photography equipment retailer from my connection with the university photographic club. Perhaps I should also mention that we did a lot of work together—you know the club is one of the biggest university photography clubs in Taiwan, with over six hundred members, so I had a really good working relationship with their boss. I knew that he was having problems with his supplier. I approached him first and asked him how much he was paying for his supplies. Then I went

to my boss at Campho and told him I thought we might get a big customer if we could beat that price. I was able to convince my boss that it would be good for business. My boss agreed, after looking at the margins, and so the retailer changed suppliers. Not only that, but he was so pleased with the deal and service he got from Campho, that he told one of his colleagues in the industry about it, and they approached me as well for the same deal. I succeeded in increasing Campho's revenues a bit. At the same time, I was successful in negotiating a cheaper price for the photographic association for our supplies. It was great synthesis; everyone benefited.

Task 4.11 ▶參考答案

　　注意，除了 set-phrases 中的動詞以外，大部分的動詞都是過去簡單式，這是因為凱文是在談論一段過去的時期，他已經不在 Campho 上班了。

　　請利用以下凱文回答的中文翻譯來檢核自己的理解力吧。

面試官：請談一談曾經得到的一個成就。

凱　文：嗯，讓我想一想。我最引以為豪的一件事，就是在 Campho 上班時為公司帶進了兩個大客戶。我經由大學攝影社的關係，認識了一家大攝影設備零售商。或許我也應該提到我和那家公司合作了很多次──你也知道，我們的攝影社是台灣最大的大學攝影社，有 600 多名會員，所以我和那家公司老闆關係很好。我知道他當時和供應商有一些問題，便主動去找他，問他付那家供應商多少錢。然後我去找我在 Campho 的老闆，告訴他如果我們出的價錢更好，我們可能就會爭取到一個大客戶。我說服老闆這樣對公司生意有好處。老闆算了一下利潤之後便同意了，所以那家零售商就換掉了供應商。不僅如此，那家公司老闆對 Campho

給他的條件和服務滿意得不得了，還跟他在業界的一個同行講了這件事情，結果那家公司也找我詢問同樣的條件。最後我成功地幫 Campho 提高了一些收入，同時也為攝影社談到了比較低的價錢，購買供給品。整個結果非常圓滿，大家都獲利。

Task 4.12

請閱讀以下黛西對一次失敗經驗的說明。找出剛學過的 set-phrases 並畫底線，然後利用下面的動詞，轉換成過去簡單式後填寫在空格中，有的動詞可以多次使用。注意這些動詞的用法。

absorb	complete	pay	take
appreciate	discover	seem	tell
be × 4	have to × 2	start	set
	learn		

Interviewer: Tell me about your biggest failure.

Daisy: Sorry I don't follow you.

Interviewer: Tell me about a mistake you made or a failure that you've had in your career.

Daisy: I'll have to think about that. OK. Well, one of my least successful experiences was when I _____ up a company for a foreign entrepreneur in Taiwan. It _____ a long time ago when I was just starting out in my first job, and I didn't really know a lot about the regulations for foreigners setting up businesses in Taiwan. I _____ all the paper work, and _____ the client's money, and then _____ him he _____ ready to start trading. He _____ his business, and all _____ to be going well. Then I _____, to my horror, that the company had not been approved, and that he was trading illegally, and what's more, that he _____ pay a fine. I _____ tell the guy, and my boss _____ furious. He

_____ very good about it, though, because he _____ the fine for the guy, and didn't take it out of my salary. He _____ the cost, which I really _____. What I should have done was to check the status of the company before telling the guy he could start trading. However, it was a positive learning experience for me. What I'm trying to say is that I _____ to double-check everything.

Task 4.12 ▶參考答案 ▶▶聽力 4.7

請閱讀下面的談話，以核對答案。各位還可利用聽力 4.7 培養臨場感。

| Interviewer: | Tell me about your biggest failure. |

| Daisy: | Sorry, I don't follow you. |

| Interviewer: | Tell me about a mistake you made or a failure that you've had in your career. |

| Daisy: | I'll have to think about that. OK. Well, one of my least successful experiences was when I set up a company for a foreign entrepreneur in Taiwan. It was a long time ago when I was just starting out in my first job, and I didn't really know a lot about the regulations for foreigners setting up businesses in Taiwan. I completed all the paper work, and took the client's money, and then told him he was ready to start trading. He started his business, and all seemed to be going well. Then I discovered, to my horror, that the company had not been approved, and that he was trading illegally, and |

what's more, that he had to pay a fine. I had to tell the guy, and my boss was furious. He was very good about it, though, because he paid the fine for the guy, and didn't take it out of my salary. He absorbed the cost, which I really appreciated. What I should have done was to check the status of the company before telling the guy he could start trading. However, it was a positive learning experience for me. What I'm trying to say is that I learned to double-check everything.

此外，也可利用以下黛西回答的中文翻譯來檢核理解力。

面試官：請談一談你最嚴重的失敗經驗。

黛　西：抱歉，我沒聽懂你的問題。

面試官：請談一談你在過去工作上犯下的一個錯誤或遭遇的一次失敗經驗。

黛　西：這我得想一想。好，我最不成功的一個經驗，就是有次幫一個外國企業家在台灣開公司。那是很久以前的事了，我才剛開始第一份工作，對外國人在台灣開公司的規定不是很了解。我完成了所有的表格文件，收了客戶的錢，然後跟他說他可以開始做貿易了。於是他就開始做生意，一切似乎都進行地很順利，後來我駭然發現他的公司並沒有被核准，等於他在非法從事貿易，更糟的是他必須付罰金。我不得不向那位客戶據實以告，我的老闆簡直氣炸了，但是老闆還是保持很好的風度，因為他幫那位客戶付了罰金，而且沒有從我薪水中扣錢。我老闆吸收了成本，我非常感激他。早知道我會先更仔細地檢查公司狀況，再告訴那位客戶可以開始做生意了。不過這件事對我來說是很正面的學習經驗。我的意思是說，我學到了凡事都得重複檢查一遍。

值得注意的是，黛西是從 One of my least successful experiences was when ... 說起，並以正面的感想作結尾，用 However, it was a positive learning experience for me 來說明她學到的教訓。

Task 4.13

請利用 set-phrases 和過去式練習說明過去的失敗經驗和成就。尚可利用 MP3 播放器錄音，確定各位在時態和 set-phrases 的使用上正確無誤。

說明職務內容

好，現在我們繼續往下研究關於職務內容的口說技巧，共分三種。

第一種是說明目前的職務，描述工作性質和日常（usually）職責。

第二種是說明目前工作上正在進行（at the moment）的業務，例如此刻正在執行的案子。這時要稍微謹慎一些，避免說出太多目前任職公司正在進行的業務，不過描述自己帶領團隊的方式是可以的，或者強調自己在目前的案子中如何運用才幹也可以。

第三種是談論過去（in the past）工作上的職責。現在我們就來看一看可以用到的 set-phrases 吧。

Task 4.14

請將以下這些 set-phrases 加以分類，寫在下頁所屬的欄位中。

I am accountable to sb. for n.p.	I was put in charge of n.p.
I am currently accountable to sb. for n.p.	I was responsible for handling n.p.
I currently have responsibility for n.p./Ving ...	I'm accountable for n.p.
I had to handle n.p.	I'm currently in charge of n.p.
I had to sort out n.p.	I'm currently responsible for handling n.p.
I have responsibility for n.p./Ving ...	I'm handling n.p.
I have to handle n.p.	I'm heading n.p.
I have to sort out n.p.	I'm in charge of n.p.
I head n.p.	I'm leading n.p.
I headed n.p.	I'm looking after n.p.
I lead n.p.	I'm managing n.p.
	I'm often/usually appointed to V ...

I led n.p.
I look after n.p.
I looked after n.p.
I manage n.p.
I managed n.p.
I'm often/usually put in charge of
n.p.
I took responsibility for n.p./Ving
I was accountable to sb. for n.p.
I was appointed to V ...
I was asked to take on n.p.
I was assigned to V ...
I was in charge of n.p.
I was made accountable for n.p.

I'm often/usually asked to take on
n.p.
I'm often/usually assigned to V ...
I'm responsible for handling n.p.
I'm sorting out n.p.
I've been appointed to V ...
I've been asked to take on n.p.
I've been assigned to V ...
I've been made accountable for n.p.
I've been put in charge of n.p.
My job at the moment is to take care
of n.p.
My job is to take care of n.p.
My job was to take care of n.p.

Describing responsibilities		
Usually	**At the moment**	**In the past**

Task　4.14　▶參考答案

請利用必備語庫 4.3 核對答案，然後閱讀語庫解析。

求職必備語庫 4.3　　▶聽力 4.8

Describing responsibilities
Usually
I have to handle n.p.
I have to sort out n.p.
I head n.p.
I look after n.p.
I manage n.p.
I lead n.p.
I have responsibility for n.p./Ving ...
I am accountable to sb. for n.p.
I'm often/usually appointed to V ...
I'm often/usually asked to take on n.p.
I'm often/usually assigned to V ...
I'm in charge of n.p.
I'm accountable for n.p.
I'm often/usually put in charge of n.p.
I'm responsible for handling n.p.
My job is to take care of n.p.
At the moment
I'm handling n.p.
I'm sorting out n.p.
I'm heading n.p.
I'm looking after n.p.
I'm managing n.p.
I'm leading n.p.

I currently have responsibility for n.p./Ving ...

I am currently accountable to sb. for n.p.

I've been appointed to V ...

I've been asked to take on n.p.

I've been assigned to V ...

I'm currently in charge of n.p.

I've been made accountable for n.p.

I've been put in charge of n.p.

I'm currently responsible for handling n.p.

My job at the moment is to take care of n.p.

In the past

I had to handle n.p.

I had to sort out n.p.

I headed n.p.

I looked after n.p.

I managed n.p.

I led n.p.

I took responsibility for n.p./Ving ...

I was accountable to sb. for n.p.

I was appointed to V ...

I was asked to take on n.p.

I was assigned to V ...

I was in charge of n.p.

I was made accountable for n.p.

I was put in charge of n.p.

I was responsible for handling n.p.

My job was to take care of n.p.

語庫解析

▶ 描述目前工作的日常職責時，主要是用現在簡單式的動詞時態，而且 set-phrases 中都會出現 often 和 usually 等詞。

▶ 描述目前進行中的案子時，應該要用現在進行式（be Ving）或現在完成式（have p.p.）。

▶ 描述過去工作的職責時，應該要用過去簡單式。

Task 4.15

請利用聽力 4.8 練習必備語庫 4.3 中 set-phrases 的發音。

Task 4.16

請將下列問題分成以下這四類：

1. 用現在簡單式回答的問題
2. 用現在進行式或現在完成式回答的問題
3. 用過去簡單式回答的問題
4. 用不同時態回答的問題

Did you increase profits or sales in your last job?	
Did you reduce costs at your last company? How did you do this?	
Do you consider yourself successful?	
Do you feel you are ready to take on a lot of responsibility?	
Do you feel you are ready to take on more responsibility?	
Do you feel you made good progress in your last job?	
Do you prefer working in a small, medium, or large company?	
Do you work well under pressure?	
Do you work well with other people? Or are you a loner?	

Explain the organizational structure of your last company and how you fitted into it	
Have you ever been fired?	
How did you get along with your previous manager/supervisor, co-workers, and subordinates?	
How good are you at managing money?	
How good are you at managing people?	
How good are you at managing stress?	
How good are you at managing your time?	
How long have you been between jobs?	
How long have you been looking for a job?	
How much does your last job resemble the one you are applying for? What are the differences?	
In your previous job what did you do on a day-to-day basis?	
Tell me about what you did in your previous job.	
Tell me something about your interests and hobbies.	
What activities did you do in college that you think have prepared you for working in a company?	
What are the differences between the job you are applying for and the last job you had?	
What are you doing at the moment?	
What are your main duties at your current job?	
What are you most proud of in your career?	
What are you working on at the moment?	
What did you learn in college?	
What did you learn in your last job?	
What have you been doing in the time between your last job and now?	
What pleased you about your last job?	
What's the best job you've ever had and why?	
Why did you choose a career in (industry, field, etc.)?	
Why did you join your previous company?	

Task 4.16 ▶參考答案

請核對答案，然後閱讀時態解析。

Did you increase profits or sales in your last job?	3
Did you reduce costs at your last company? How did you do this?	3
Do you consider yourself successful?	4
Do you feel you are ready to take on a lot of responsibility?	4
Do you feel you are ready to take on more responsibility?	4
Do you feel you made good progress in your last job?	3
Do you prefer working in a small, medium, or large company?	4
Do you work well under pressure?	4
Do you work well with other people? Or are you a loner?	4
Explain the organizational structure of your last company and how you fitted into it	3
Have you ever been fired?	3
How did you get along with your previous manager/supervisor, co-workers, and subordinates?	3
How good are you at managing money?	4
How good are you at managing people?	4
How good are you at managing stress?	4
How good are you at managing your time?	4
How long have you been between jobs?	2
How long have you been looking for a job?	2
How much does your last job resemble the one you are applying for? What are the differences?	3
In your previous job what did you do on a day-to-day basis?	3
Tell me about what you did in your previous job.	3
Tell me something about your interests and hobbies.	1
What activities did you do in college that you think have prepared you for working in a company?	3

What are the differences between the job you are applying for and the last job you had?	4
What are you doing at the moment?	2
What are your main duties at your current job?	1
What are you most proud of in your career?	3
What are you working on at the moment?	2
What did you learn in college?	3
What did you learn in your last job?	3
What have you been doing in the time between your last job and now?	2
What pleased you about your last job?	3
What's the best job you've ever had and why?	3, 2
Why did you choose a career in (industry, field, etc.)?	3
Why did you join your previous company?	3

時態解析

▶ 回答第四類問題的時候，建議你舉出一些例子，用過去簡單動詞具體描述過去工作中做過的事情，或者用現在進行式或現在完成式具體描述現在工作中做的事情。我們來看一些範例吧。

Task 4.17 ▶ 聽力 4.9   42

　　請閱讀下面凱文和黛西的回答範例，從中找出必備語庫 4.3 的 set-phrases，並劃上底線。請記得利用聽力 4.9 培養臨場感。

Interviewer:	Do you work well under pressure?

Kevin:	Sorry, I don't follow you.

Interviewer: Can you cope with stress and pressure if things get extremely busy?

Kevin: Well, I think I can manage pressure. For example, I started working for Campho before the end of the semester, so I was still studying for my final exams. I managed to get good grades on my exams and learn all about the new job, the products, the customers, and so on. I also had to handle a big order right from the beginning. So, yes, I think I'm used to pressure.

Interviewer: Do you consider yourself successful?

Daisy: Well it depends what you mean by successful, doesn't it? I'm good at my job and I think I'm an asset to anyone that hires me. For instance, in my current job, I'm looking after three major clients. I'm leading a team of eight people, and I've been assigned to train the new intake on client management. So I think I'm good at what I do. And I enjoy it. I think that probably makes me successful, right?

Task **4.17** ▶參考答案

　　注意凱文在答覆對方問題時，會舉出過去工作上的一些實例，而黛西在答覆對方問題時，則是舉出目前工作上的一些實例。可參考以下凱文和黛西回答的中文翻譯來檢核自己的理解力。

　　面試官：你抗壓性強嗎？

凱　　文：抱歉，我沒聽懂你的問題。

面試官：在極度忙碌的情況之下，你能不能應付壓力？

凱　　文：嗯，我覺得我可以應付壓力。舉一個例子，我是在學期末開始在 Campho 上班，所以當時還在準備期末考。我考試還是取得了好成績，同時也全面了解了新工作、產品、客戶等。我從一開始就必須處理大宗訂單。所以我覺得我很適應壓力。

面試官：你覺得自己成功嗎？

黛　　西：這得看你對成功的定義是什麼，對不對？我對自己的工作很在行，也覺得自己對任何雇主來說都是一個資產。舉例而言，在現在的工作中我管理三個重要客戶，而且既是一個八人小組的組長，也被指派負責訓練新人客戶管理。所以我覺得對自己的工作很在行，而且樂在其中，我覺得這大概就算是成功了吧，對不對？

Task 4.18 ▶聽力 4.10

請聽聽力 4.10 中的問題，這些問題和 Task 4.16 的問題一致，只是順序不同。請在聽完每個問題之後先按暫停，試著自己回答，並錄下答案，以供播聽改進。

Task 4.18 ▶參考答案

▶ 如同之前做過的練習，MP3 中的問題和 Task 4.16 的順序不同。請盡量快速地回答問題，不要停頓太久才開口回答。

▶ 聽一下自己使用 set-phrases 的方式。語調是否有明顯的抑揚頓挫？聽起來夠流利嗎？你能如何回答得更好？

好，我們已經學會用英文談論過去和現在工作上的職務，接下來該學習如何談論未來的生涯規畫了。

談論未來的生涯規畫

　　談到未來的生涯規畫時最好不要講得太明白。舉個例子，如果面試官問你對未來有什麼樣的生涯規畫，你卻回答你計畫三年後暫時放下工作去攻讀碩士學位或者生小孩，對方可能覺得你在公司只會待三年，便決定不僱用你了。

　　談到未來生涯的時候只要說明基本的願望和大概的期望即可，不需要講得過於具體。現在來研究這種時候可以派上用場的 set-phrases 吧。

Task 4.19

請看以下用於討論未來生涯規畫的 set-phrases。利用聽力 4.11 練習發音。

求 職 必 備 語 庫 4.4　　▶ 聽力 4.11　　

Talking about your future	
I'd like to V ...	What I'd like to do is V ...
I'm hoping to V ...	I need to gain some experience in n.p.
I'm hoping that + clause.	I want to V ...
I hope to V ...	I really want to V ...
I want the chance to V ...	I'm looking for n.p.

Task 4.20

請利用剛學過的 set-phrases 練習回答下面的問題。

- ❏ Are you prepared to relocate?
- ❏ Are you willing to travel abroad?
- ❏ How long do you think you will stay in this job?
- ❏ What are you looking for in a new job?
- ❏ What are your career aims?

☐ What can we offer that your previous company cannot offer?

☐ What level of salary are you looking for now?

☐ What would your ideal job be?

☐ What's your career plan?

☐ Why are you changing careers?

Task 4.21 ▶聽力 4.12

　　請閱讀下面凱文和黛西的回答範例，從中找出必備語庫 4.4 的 set-phrases，並畫上底線。請利用聽力 4.12 培養臨場感。

Interviewer:	What are your career aims?

Kevin:	Well, first I'd like to get some experience from the real work world. Let's put it this way: I know that my experience is only limited to vacation jobs, and although I've done quite well so far, I want the chance to develop something a bit more permanent and long-term. I mean, what I'd like to do is get to a mid-level management position as soon as possible.

Interviewer:	What are you looking for in a new job?

Daisy:	Yes, good question. Umm, well, I'm looking for a new challenge. I've had quite a good career so far, things have worked out well, and I've learned a lot. However, I still want to learn more. Let me rephrase what I just said. I'm hoping to fill the gaps in my experience. For example, I'm hoping to get a position with more strategic responsibility.

Task **4.21** ▶參考答案

請參考以下凱文和黛西回答的中文翻譯來檢核理解力。

面試官：你的事業目標為何？

凱　文：嗯，我希望先得到職場上真實世界的一些經驗。這麼說吧，我知道我的經驗只限於假期打工，雖然目前為止我做的還不錯，我希望有機會建立更永久和長期的工作經驗。我的意思是說，我是想盡快做到中級主管職位。

面試官：你對新工作有什麼期望？

黛　西：是的，好問題。呃，我希望有新的挑戰。目前為止我已經擁有不錯的事業，一切都滿順利的，也學到了很多，但是我還是想再多學一點。我換個方式說吧。我希望填補空白的經驗。例如，我想負責策略性比較高的職位。

應付負面問題

在應付負面的問題時，必備語庫 4.4 中的一些 set-phrases 也可派上用場，我們接下來就來學習相關的用法。

Task 4.22

請看以下問題，試著找出這些問題有何共同點？

> ▶ Did your previous company live up to your expectations?
> ▶ How do you feel about working long hours of overtime with no pay?
> ▶ How many hours are you prepared to work?
> ▶ How often are you off sick?
> ▶ What annoyed you about your last job?
> ▶ What do you dislike about the job you have applied for?
> ▶ What do you dislike doing?
> ▶ What do you think of your last company?
> ▶ What would you like to avoid in your next job?
> ▶ What's the worst job you've ever had and why?
> ▶ Why are you leaving your current company now?
> ▶ Why are you leaving your current job?
> ▶ Would you compete for my job?

Task 4.22 ▶參考答案

這些問題的共同點在於都具有引導作用，企圖讓你說出負面的感想來。這類負面問題對面試官來說很重要，他們可以藉機觀察你應付負面話題的反應。舉例來說，如果你把過去的工作說得很差，面試官可能會覺得你是個麻煩人物。

遇到這種問題的應對方法，就是用 set-phrases 簡短地說一下負面的感想，後面就會爲各位介紹這種 set-phrases。接下來，各位應該馬上運用必備語庫 4.4 中的 set-phrases 練習談論正面的感想。

我們來看一看凱文和黛西如何應付這類問題吧。

Task 4.23 ▶聽力 4.13

請閱讀以下回應，並播放聽力 4.13 培養臨場感。試著找出這些答覆的共同點。

Interviewer:	What annoyed you about your previous job?

Kevin:	Well, the training could have been handled better. For the first few days, I was really confused because there didn't seem to be anyone whose job it was to tell me what to do, or show me what was expected of me. But I guess you guys will cover that in the training you offer. I'm hoping that I can get the hang of the new job as quickly as possible with support, so that I can start to make a positive contribution.

Interviewer:	What would you like to avoid in your next job?

Daisy:	I'd like to avoid overlapping lines of communication. In my previous job there wasn't a clear distinction about whom I should be reporting to—the finance director, or the client service director—so sometimes things were not as efficient as they could have been. I'm looking for a clear chain of command so that messages and directions don't get lost.

Task 4.23 ▶參考答案

　　這兩個答覆都是以負面的感想說起，但後來卻轉而談論正面的感想。凱文說公司的訓練沒有盡善盡美，黛西則說她之前工作的溝通管道不是很清楚，希望下一份工作能避免同樣的問題。

　　凱文表示希望新的工作能很快上手，這樣的回答非常正面，因為他把重點放在對新工作的期望，而不是批評之前的工作。黛西表示希望有清楚的溝通管道；她也是把重點放在對新工作的期望，而沒有說希望避免什麼樣的問題。

　　各位有沒有注意到，凱文和黛西都是利用必備語庫 4.4 中的 set-phrases，將負面的事情扭轉成正面的事情？凱文是說 I'm hoping that + clause，而黛西是說 I'm looking for n.p.。請參考以下凱文和黛西回答的中文翻譯來檢核自己的理解力吧。

面試官：你之前的工作有什麼困擾你的地方？

凱　文：嗯，員工培訓應該再好一些。剛開始的幾天我都搞不清楚狀況，因為好像沒有人負責跟我說明，或告訴我該做什麼。但是我想你們在訓練新人的時候都會涵蓋這些事情。我希望在有人的協助之下能盡快掌握新工作，開始有所貢獻。

面試官：你希望在新工作中避免什麼事情？

黛　西：我想避免溝通責任上發生重疊的狀況。在之前的工作中，公司沒有明白規定我的上司是誰：到底是財務部主管還是客服主管，所以有時辦事效率不是很理想。我希望清楚知道我的上司是誰，以免錯失訊息和指示。

現在我們來看一下討論負面感想的語彙。

Task 4.24

請看以下必備語庫 4.5 中的 set-phrases，並利用聽力 4.14 練習發音。

求職必備語庫 4.5　▶ 聽力 4.14　

Responding to negative questions

... could have been better.

... could have been more adj.

I was dissatisfied with n.p.

I was dissatisfied with the fact that + clause.

I was less than happy about n.p.

I was less than happy about the fact that + clause.

I'd like to avoid n.p. /Ving ...

Sometimes things were not as adj. as they could have been.

There could have been more n.p.

There didn't seem to be n.p.

There was a lack of n.p.

There wasn't enough n.p.

Task 4.25

請回到前面看 Task 4.23 的回答，仔細觀察其中有多少用詞是出自必備語庫 4.5 的 set-phrases，以及這些用來回答負面問題 set-phrases 的用法。

Task 4.26

現在請練習回答 Task 4.22 中的問題。用 MP3 錄音器錄下答覆，並注意回答的內容是否正面。

截至目前爲止我們學到的語彙都著重於解釋工作經驗、資歷和未來生涯規畫，現在我們要來學習一些 set-phrases，用於和面試官互動和組織答覆。

與面試官互動及組織答覆

建構答案的時候，應該用 set-phrases 補充內容（add information），讓面試官知道你還沒有講完，並表現出組織想法的卓越邏輯能力。

如果聽不懂問題，不要擔心，只要向面試官請求重複問題（asking for repetition）或換句話說即可。

如果你覺得自己表達得不是很清楚，或者從面試官的臉色看起來好像沒有聽懂你的回答，這時最好重新表達（re-expressing yourself）一次。

如果面試官問你一個艱澀的問題，或者出乎意料之外甚或沒準備到的問題，則應該拖延時間（buying time），同時思考如何回答對方。

現在我們就來學習用於這種情況的 set-phrases 吧。

Task 4.27

請將以下這些 set-phrases 加以分類，寫在下頁所屬的欄位中。

Also, ...	Perhaps I should also mention that + clause.
And another thing, ...	Sorry, I don't follow you.
As well as this, ...	Sorry, I didn't catch the last part of what you said.
Don't misunderstand me, ...	
For example, ...	Sorry, would you mind repeating that?
For instance, ...	Hmm. That's a difficult one.
How can I put it?	Well, it depends what you mean by ..., doesn't it?
How should I put it?	
I mean, ...	Well, let me see.
I'll have to think about that.	Well, let me think now.
If I said that, I didn't mean ...	

Just a small point, ...	What I mean is ...
Let me put it another way.	What I meant was ...
Let me rephrase what I just said.	What I'm saying is ...
	What I'm trying to say is ...
Let's put it this way:	What was the question again?
Not only that, but also ...	What's more, ...
Oh, I almost forgot.	Yes, good question. Umm, ...
	You know, ...

Adding things

Asking for repetition

Re-expressing yourself

Buying time

Task 4.27 ▶參考答案

請利用下面的必備語庫核對答案。

 ▶聽力 4.15　　　　　　　　　　　　　　　

Organizing your response and interacting with the interviewer

Adding things

Also, ...	Not only that, but also ...
And another thing, ...	Oh, I almost forgot ...
As well as this, ...	Perhaps I should also mention that +
Just a small point, ...	clause.
For example, ...	For instance, ...
What's more, ...	

Asking for repetition

Sorry, I don't follow you.

Sorry, I didn't catch the last part of what you said.

Sorry, would you mind repeating that?

What was the question again?

Re-expressing yourself

Let me put it another way.	If I said that, I didn't mean ...
Let me rephrase what I just said.	What I mean is ...
Let's put it this way:	What I meant was ...
Don't misunderstand me, ...	What I'm saying is ...
How shall I put it?	What I'm trying to say is ...
I mean, ...	You know, ...

Buying time

Well, let me see.	I'll have to think about that.
Well, let me think now.	Yes, good question. Umm, ...
How should I put it?	How can I put it?
Hmm. That's a difficult one.	Well, it depends what you mean by
	..., doesn't it?

Task 4.28

請利用聽力 4.15 練習必備語庫 4.6 中 set-phrases 的發音。

Task 4.29

請回到前面重新閱讀 Task 4.5 和 4.6 、 Task 4.11 和 4.12 、 Task 4. 17 和 4.21 和 4.23 的回答範例,並同時播放聽力部分,將聽到必備語庫 4.6 的 set-phrases 找出來、畫上底線,然後研究用法。

Task 4.29 ▶參考答案

請重複練習幾次,直到所有的 set-phrases 都找齊了為止。

Task 4.30 ▶聽力 4.16

請利用聽力 4.16 的問題練習自己回答。並可試著運用必備語庫 4.6 中的 set-phrases ,或其他在本單元中學到的適當語彙。

> ❑ Can you act on your own initiative?
> ❑ Can you motivate other people?
> ❑ How do you chair a meeting?
> ❑ How long do you think it would be before you were making a significant contribution to our team?
> ❑ How long do you think you would stay in this job?

接下來,讓我們來學習如何向面試官發問吧。

發問與積極傾聽

面試到了尾聲的時候，面試官會問你有沒有任何問題。這時你要是說沒有問題可就大錯特錯了，即使趕時間或覺得對方在趕時間都不能說沒有問題。面試官給你機會提問的目的有二。

第一，他想提供你需要的資訊，讓你對工作的內容具備清楚的概念。第二，他想聽聽看你會問出什麼樣的問題。面試官可以透過你的問題判斷你這個人。例如你要是馬上就詢問薪水和規定，你可能就會給人只在乎金錢的印象。即使你的確只在乎金錢，這種表現也不會提高你爭取到工作的機會！反過來，如果你是問公司目前面對的一些問題和因應策略，那麼面試官就會覺得你有興趣多了解公司和公司的問題，對公司可能會有寶貴的貢獻。

由此推論，你在問問題時也應該有兩個目的。第一，取得之前對工作沒有的相關資訊。第二，用問題來博取面試官對你的好感。

在面試之前，一定要仔細思考什麼問題才能深得面試官的心。現在我們就來學習用於提出聰明問題的語彙吧。

Task 4.31

請看以下這些詢問資訊的 set-phrases，並用聽力 4.17 練習發音。

求職必備語庫 4.7 ▶ 聽力 4.17

Asking questions	
I'd like to know + wh-clause.	Do you know + wh-clause?
I'm interested in X. Can you tell me more about this?	Could I ask about n.p.?
	Could I ask + wh-clause?
Could you tell me + wh-clause?	
Could you tell me something about n.p.?	

Task **4.32** ▶聽力 4.18

請看以下凱文和黛西提出的問題，他們想了解 Unit 3 中所應徵的工作。並可利用聽力 4.18 練習如何實際提出這些問題。

Kevin: I'd like to know how you deal with the government regulations in China. How much freedom of movement do you have in that market with your products?

Could you tell me something about your midterm strategy in the China market?

Could I ask about relations between Chinese staff and foreign staff, especially relations between Taiwanese and Mainland Chinese staff?

Daisy: I'm interested in the IMF's position on loan defaults from Africa. Can you tell me more about this?

Could I ask why a knowledge of Mandarin and Cantonese is essential for this job?

Could you tell me what projects the IMF is currently pursuing?

Task **4.32** ▶參考答案

請參考以下凱文和黛西提出問題的中文翻譯來檢核自己的理解力。

凱　文：　我想了解你們如何因應中國政府的規定。在中國市場中，你們產品流通有多大的自由度？

你能不能說明一下你們在中國市場的中期策略？

我能不能問一下中國員工和外國員工的關係，尤其是台灣和中國大陸員工之間的關係？

黛　西：　我有興趣了解國際貨幣基金會對非洲不能償還貸款的看法。你能不能進一步說明？

我能不能了解一下，為什麼國語和廣東話對這個工作而言很重要？

能不能請你說明，國際貨幣基金會目前的業務？

聽面試官回答你的問題的時候，務必要積極地傾聽，也就是說在面試官講話的時候應該有所回應，例如在面試官講完一句話的時候，趁機插入一些詞或短的 set-phrases。

不要只是安安靜靜地聽，最好也做一些筆記，讓面試官知道你對他的答覆非常感興趣。

以下提供一些 set-phrases，在面試官回答你的問題時可以使用，讓對方知道你很專心地在聽他說話。

Task 4.33

請看以下字詞和 set-phrases，你可以在聽對方說話時用上幾句。利用聽力 4.19 學習發音。

求 職 必 備 語 庫 4.8　▶ 聽力 4.19　52

Listening actively		
Right.	Oh yes?	Mmm.
OK.	Indeed.	Is that right?
Yes.	Absolutely.	I see.
And?	Uh huh.	Really?
Quite.		

Task **4.34** ▶ 聽力 4.20

請聽聽力 4.20 中面試官對 Task 4.32 中問題的回答。一邊聽一邊用必備語庫 4.8 中的語彙練習回應面試官。

以下提供凱文和黛西個別提出的問題及面試官的答覆對照文。

Kevin:	Could I ask about relations between Chinese staff and foreign staff, especially relations between Taiwanese and Mainland Chinese staff?
Interviewer:	Well, generally speaking, I have to say that relations between Taiwanese and Mainland Chinese staff are usually very good. There's often some initial curiosity, but that soon dies down. As long as both sides stick to the job, and in getting to know each other, there should be no problems. We've found that it's always best to avoid any kind of political remarks or discussions to keep things running smoothly and keep the staff on good terms with each other. We take this very seriously at GGM.
Daisy:	Could I ask why a knowledge of Mandarin and Cantonese is essential for this job?
Interviewer:	Well, that's a good question. The IMF is getting more closely involved with China as China moves towards liberalizing its financial markets. The exchange rate issue is big on the agenda, as you know, and once China liberalizes their financial markets and unpegs

the yuan, opportunities for foreign investors in the Chinese financial markets will increase. It's important for the IMF to be involved at the ground level so that we can influence things in the right way, the way that's safe and sound for China's trading partners, and ulti-mately, of course, for the global economy. That's why we need more Mandarin and Cantonese speakers on the staff.

Task 4.34 ▶參考答案

請參考以下凱文和黛西個別提出的問題，及其面試官答覆的中文翻譯來檢核理解力。

凱　文：我能不能了解一下中國員工和外國員工的關係，尤其是台灣和中國大陸員工？

面試官：嗯，一般來說，我是覺得通常台灣和中國大陸員工之間的關係都很好。往往一開始時會有一些好奇，但是很快就熟稔起來了。只要雙方專注在工作上和盡量了解對方，應該就沒有問題。我們發現最好是避免任何政治性言論或討論，事情就會進行地比較順暢，員工彼此也能維持良好的關係。我們通用汽車非常重視這一點。

黛　西：我能不能了解一下，爲什麼國語和廣東話對這個工作而言很重要？

面試官：嗯，這個問題很好。國際貨幣基金會和中國的關係越來越密切，因爲中國正朝著開放金融市場的方向前進。匯率問題是計畫中的大目標，你也知道，一旦中國開放了金融市場和解除對人民幣的管制，外國投資公司在中國金融市場的機會就會提高。對國際貨幣基金會而言，很重要的一點就是從基層開始參與，這樣我們就可以適當地影響政策，爲中國的貿易夥伴奠定良好和安全的基礎，最終當然也是爲了全球經濟著想。這就是爲什麼我們需要更多會說國語和廣東話的員工。

　　好了，面試方面的教學到此結束。在學習結束之前，請回到本單元前面的學習清單，瀏覽一遍確定所有的項目都確實了解了。

　　最後，我要給你一個基本的建議：記住，多多練習，尤其是 set-phrases 的發音和準確度。如果你的詞彙準備充分，按照我在上一個單元中給你的建議做好準備，也運用了我在本單元中教你的 set-phrases 和訣竅，你在面試時的表現應該非常優秀而且自信滿滿。

　　不論你找的是什麼工作，祝你馬到成功！

Plus +

附錄
Appendices

附錄一：後續電子郵件

　　建議各位在面試過後隔天寄一封電子郵件給面試官，感謝對方撥冗與你見面和進行面試，此外，可在信中提到一些在面試時討論過的事項，最後記得要向對方表示期待能再進一步連絡。

　　以下提供一封電子郵件的範本給各位參考。

Dear ____(interviewer's name here)____ ,

Just a quick note to thank you for taking the time to meet with me yesterday.

I was very interested in what you had to say about (word partnership here) , and hope we can talk more about this in the future.

In the meantime, if you have any questions or need any further information about my work history, please do not hesitate to contact me.

Once again, many thanks.

Best regards,

____(your name here)____

____（面試官的名字）____ 您好：

謹以此信感謝您昨日撥冗與我面談。

我對您提到的 ____（這裡填入 word partnership）____ 深感興趣，希望未來有機會能與您進一步討論。

在此期間，如您對我過去的資歷有任何疑問或需要詳細資料，請與我聯絡，不必客氣。

再次感謝。

____（你的名字）____ 敬上

　　我們來看一看凱文和黛西在歷經 Unit 4 的面試實戰之後，如何運用這封後續電子郵件向面試官表示感謝。此外，各位也可利用 MP3 中的有聲版後續電子郵件，來練習口語上的致謝。

Dear Mr. Roberts,

Just a quick note to thank you for taking the time to meet with me yesterday.

I was very interested in what you had to say about relations between Mainland Chinese and Taiwanese staff, and hope we can talk more about this in the future.

In the meantime, if you have any questions or need any further information about my work history, please do not hesitate to contact me.

Once again, many thanks.

Best regards,

Kevin Gao

羅勃茲先生，您好：

謹以此信感謝您昨日撥冗與我面談。

我對您提到的中國大陸員工和台灣員工之間的關係深感興趣，希望未來有機會能與您進一步討論。

在此期間，如您對我過去的資歷有任何疑問或需要詳細資料，請與我聯絡，不必客氣。

再次感謝。

高凱文敬上

Dear Ms. Jones,

Just a quick note to thank you for taking the time to meet with me yesterday.

I was very interested in what you had to say about the IMF's role in the emerging financial markets in China, and hope we can talk more about this in the future.

In the meantime, if you have any questions or need any further information about my work history, please do not hesitate to contact me.

Once again, many thanks.

Best regards,

Daisy Wang

瓊絲女士，您好：

謹以此信感謝您昨日撥冗與我面談。

我對您提到的國際金融組織在中國新興的金融市場所扮演的角色深感興趣，希望未來有機會能與您進一步討論。

在此期間，如您對我過去的資歷有任何疑問或需要詳細資料，請與我聯絡，不必客氣。

再次感謝。

王黛西敬上

附錄二：求職必備語庫

求職必備語庫 1.1 　03

active	活躍的	keen	熱衷的
caring	有愛心的	kind	親切的
committed	堅定的	knowledgeable	博學的
compassionate	有同情心的	mature	成熟的
considerate	周到的	productive	多產的
creative	有創意的	qualified	合格的
dedicated	專注的	reliable	可信賴的
devoted	專心致志的	resourceful	資源豐富的
dynamic	有活力的	responsible	負責任的
energetic	精力旺盛的	skilled	有技能的
enthusiastic	熱心的	stable	穩定的
experienced	經驗豐富的	steady	沉著的
inventive	善於創造的	trustworthy	可信的
dependable	可靠的		

求職必備語庫 1.2 　04

accounting	computing	legal	public sector
advertising	financial	manufacturing	research
agricultural	HR	marketing	sales
banking	insurance	medical	telemarketing
business	IT	pharmaceutical	tourism

求職必備語庫 1.3 　05

... (special) responsibility for ...	... all aspects of ...
... in a broad range of areas ...	... experience of ...
... with (special) expertise in ...	... as well as ...
... experience includes ...	... with a commitment to ...
... including ...	... (special) emphasis on ...
... with almost ...	... reporting to ...
... current interest in ...	... much of it ...
... current work in ...	... with more than ...
... many aspects of ...	... many of them ...

1. Statement of purpose 表明來意

I am writing in connection with n.p.

I'm writing to apply for the position of n.p.

I am writing in the hope that you have a vacancy for a n.p. in your n.p.

I am writing in the hope that you have a vacant position for a n.p. in your n.p.

2. Introduction 自我介紹

You will see from my attached CV that + clause.

I also have extensive experience with n.p.

I already have some experience with this.

I am interested in Ving ...

I would like to extend my experience of n.p.

3. Current situation 現況

I am currently Ving ...

At the moment I am working as a n.p.

For the last two years I have been Ving ...

My present position involves Ving ...

My job here includes Ving ...

I have been able to V ...

This has resulted in n.p.

4. Work history 工作經驗

While at n.p., my duties included Ving ...

I was able to V ...

From X to X I worked as a n.p. at n.p.

My job there was to V ...

My main duties were to V ...

Among my duties in my previous job were Ving and Ving ...

5. Conclusion 結論

I believe I am suitably qualified and experienced for the job advertised.

I would welcome the opportunity to talk with you further about what opportunities you have.

I would be interested in talking with you further about what opportunities you have.

I believe I would be a suitable addition to your team.

求職必備語庫 2.2

1. Completed successfully 成功完成

Achieved sth.	Instituted sth.
Attained sth.	Negotiated sth.
Brought in sth.	Organized sth.
Built up sth.	Originated sth.
Consolidated sth.	Pioneered sth.
Created sth.	Produced sth.
Established sth.	Programmed sth.
Executed sth.	Reduced sth. (by number)
Expedited sth.	Revitalized sth.
Founded sth.	Set up sth.
Generated sth.	Shaped sth.
Improved sth.	Sold sth.
Increased sth. (by number)	Spearheaded sth.
Influenced sth.	Strengthened sth.
Initiated sth.	Systematized sth.

2. Solved a problem 解決問題

Addressed sth.	Remolded sth.
Diagnosed sth. as sth.	Reorganized sth.
Evaluated sth.	Repaired sth.
Examined sth.	Resolved sth.
Identified sth.	Reviewed sth.
Improved sth.	Revitalized sth.
Investigated sth.	Solved sth.
Overhauled sth.	Strengthened sth.
Reduced sth. (by number)	Upgraded sth.
Rehabilitated sth.	

3. Managed people 管理團隊

Appraised sth.	Managed sth.
Arbitrated (between sth. and) sth.	Mediated between X and Y
Chaired sth.	Moderated sth.
Coached sb. on sth.	Motivated sb. to V
Counseled sb. on sth.	Oversaw sth.
Delegated sth. to sb.	Recruited sb.
Directed sth.	Supervised sth.
Guided sb.	Taught sb.
Had overall responsibility for sth.	Trained sb.
Interviewed sb.	(was) Responsible for sth.
Lectured on sth.	Enlisted sb. to V
Led sth.	

4. Worked with people 合作經驗

Advised on sth.	Corresponded with sb. about sth.
Assisted in sth.	Listened to sb.
Collaborated on sth. with sb.	Negotiated with sb. on
Consulted with sb. on sth.	Persuaded sb. to V
Contracted sb. to V	Participated in sth.
Convinced sb. to V	Facilitated in sth.
Coordinated with sb. to V	

5. Handled money 掌理財務

Allocated sth. (to sth.)	Calculated sth.
Audited sth.	Forecasted sth.
Balanced sth.	Projected sth.
Budgeted sth.	

6. Handled data　整理資料

Analyzed sth.	Compiled sth.
Catalogued sth.	Formulated sth.
Clarified sth.	Prioritized sth.
Classified sth.	Projected sth.
Collected sth.	Researched sth.

7. Worked on a project　經辦案子

Anticipated sth.	Engineered sth.	Prepared sth. (for sb.)
Approved sth.	Focused on sth.	Presented sth. to sb.
Arranged sth.	Handled sth.	Prioritized sth.
Assembled sth.	Implemented sth.	Promoted sth.
Assessed sth.	Inspected sth.	Publicized sth.
Authored sth.	Integrated sth.	Recommended sth.
Carried out sth.	Introduced sth. into sth.	Reported sth.
Customized sth.	Invented sth.	Represented sth.
Dealt with sth.	Kept up sth.	Scheduled sth.
Demonstrated sth.	Maintained sth.	Took care of sth.
Designed sth.	Marketed sth.	Translated sth.
Developed sth.	Operated sth.	Worked on sth.
Drafted sth.	Performed sth.	Wrote sth.
Edited sth.	Planned sth.	

求職必備語庫 2.3

連接子句	連接子句
... and ...	At the same time, ...
... also ...	Apart from this, ...
... and also ...	As well as this, ...
... both n.p./Ving/clause and n.p./Ving/clause.	In addition, ...
... as well as n.p./Ving ...	In addition to this, ...

求職必備語庫 4.1 34

Talking modestly about yourself 謙遜談論自己

I always aim for n.p.	I think I'm quite adj.
I always aim to V ...	I think my strengths are ...
I always give my all to n.p.	I'm committed to n.p./Ving ...
I always go for n.p.	I'm told that I'm ...
I always insist on n.p.	I've been told that I'm ...
I always try to V ...	It's often said of me that I'm ...
I think I'm effective at n.p./Ving ...	People say that I'm ...
I think I'm good at n.p./Ving ...	

Giving your opinion 發表看法

As far as I can make out, ...	In my experience, ...
As I see it, ...	In my opinion, ...
From my point of view, ...	In my view, ...
I believe ...	It seems to me that ...
I firmly believe ...	My own view is that ...
I personally think ...	My position is that ...
I reckon ...	My view is that ...
I suspect that ...	There's no doubt in my mind that ...
I think ...	To my mind, ...
I'd say that ...	To my way of thinking, ...
I'm convinced that ...	

求[職][必][備][語][庫] 4.2　　　　　

Talking about successes　談論成就

I had some success at Ving ...

I managed to V ...

I succeeded in Ving ...

One of the things I'm most proud of is n.p.

I successfully managed to V ...

I was able to V ...

I was successful in Ving ...

One of the things I'm most proud of is the way that + clause.

Talking about failures　談論失敗經驗

However, I learned a lot about n.p.

However, it was a positive learning experience for me.

One of my least successful experiences was n.p.

I didn't really know n.p.

I could have done better at Ving ...

I could have done better to V ...

I didn't manage to V ...

Unfortunately, I wasn't able to V ...

One of my least successful experiences was when + clause.

What I should have done was + clause.

求 職 必 備 語 庫 4.3

Describing responsibilities 說明職務內容

Usually 日常職責

I have to handle n.p.

I have to sort out n.p.

I head n.p.

I look after n.p.

I manage n.p.

I lead n.p.

I have responsibility for n.p./Ving ...

I am accountable to sb. for n.p.

I'm often/usually appointed to V ...

I'm often/usually asked to take on n.p.

I'm often/usually assigned to V ...

I'm in charge of n.p.

I'm accountable for n.p.

I'm often/usually put in charge of n.p.

I'm responsible for handling n.p.

My job is to take care of n.p.I'm handling n.p.

At the moment 目前業務

I'm sorting out n.p.

I'm heading n.p.

I'm looking after n.p.

I'm managing n.p.

I'm leading n.p.

I currently have responsibility for n.p./Ving ...

I am currently accountable to sb. for n.p.

I've been appointed to V ...

I've been asked to take on n.p.

I've been assigned to V ...

I'm currently in charge of n.p.

I've been made accountable for n.p.

I've been put in charge of n.p.

I'm currently responsible for handling n.p.

My job at the moment is to take care of n.p.

In the past 過去職責

I had to handle n.p.

I had to sort out n.p.

I headed n.p.

I looked after n.p.

I managed n.p.

I led n.p.

I took responsibility for n.p./Ving ...

I was accountable to sb. for n.p.

I was appointed to V ...

I was asked to take on n.p.

I was assigned to V ...

I was in charge of n.p.

I was made accountable for n.p.

I was put in charge of n.p.

I was responsible for handling n.p.

My job was to take care of n.p.

求職必備語庫 4.4

Talking about your future 談論未來規畫

I'd like to V ...

I'm hoping to V ...

I'm hoping that + clause.

I hope to V ...

I want the chance to V ...

What I'd like to do is V ...

I need to gain some experience in n.p.

I want to V ...

I really want to V ...

I'm looking for n.p.

Responding to negative questions 應付負面問題

... could have been better.

... could have been more adj.

I was dissatisfied with n.p.

I was dissatisfied with the fact that + clause.

I was less than happy about n.p.

I was less than happy about the fact that + clause.

I'd like to avoid n.p. /Ving ...

Sometimes things were not as adj. as they could have been.

There could have been more n.p.

There did't seem to be n.p.

There was a lack of n.p.

There wasn't enough n.p.

與面試官互動與組織答覆

Adding things 補充內容

Also, ...

And another thing, ...

As well as this, ...

Just a small point, ...

For example, ...

What's more, ...

Not only that, but also ...

Oh, I almost forgot ...

Perhaps I should also mention that + clause.

For instance, ...

Asking for repetition 請求重述

Sorry, I don't follow you.

Sorry, I didn't catch the last part of what you said.

Sorry, would you mind repeating that?

What was the question again?

Re-expressing yourself　重新表達

Let me put it another way.	If I said that, I didn't mean ...
Let me rephrase what I just said.	What I mean is ...
Let's put it this way:	What I meant was ...
Don't misunderstand me, ...	What I'm saying is ...
How shall I put it?	What I'm trying to say is ...
I mean, ...	You know, ...

Buying time　拖延時間

Well, let me see.	I'll have to think about that.
Well, let me think now.	Yes, good question. Umm, ...
How should I put it?	How can I put it?
Hmm. That's a difficult one.	Well, it depends what you mean by ..., doesn't it?

求職必備語庫 4.7　

Asking questions　發問

I'd like to know + wh-clause.	Do you know + wh-clause?
I'm interested in X. Can you tell me more about this?	Could I ask about n.p.?
	Could I ask + wh-clause?
Could you tell me + wh-clause?	
Could you tell me something about n.p.?	

求職必備語庫 4.8　

Listening actively　積極傾聽

Right.	Oh yes?	Mmm.
OK.	Indeed.	Is that right?
Yes.	Absolutely.	I see.
And?	Uh huh.	Really?
Quite.		

 附錄三：履歷表格式

Telephone:	Email:
Date of Birth:	Nationality:
PROFILE	
EDUCATION	

WORK EXPERIENCE

OTHER ACTIVITIES

RELEVANT SKILLS

HOBBIES AND INTERESTS

國家圖書館出版品預行編目資料

愈忙愈要學求職英文 ＝ Biz English for Busy People:
job hunting / Quentin Brand作；金振寧譯.
－－初版. －－臺北市；貝塔，2007〔民96〕
面： 公分

ISBN 978-957-729-642-9（平裝附光碟片）

1. 英國語言－應用文 2. 履歷表 3. 面試

805.179 96003977

愈忙愈要學求職英文
Biz English for Busy People—Job Hunting

作　　者 / Quentin Brand
譯　　者 / 金振寧
執行編輯 / 胡元媛

出　　版 / 貝塔出版有限公司
地　　址 / 台北市100館前路12號11樓
電　　話 / (02)2314-2525
傳　　真 / (02)2312-3535
郵　　撥 / 19493777貝塔出版有限公司
客服專線 / (02)2314-3535
客服信箱 / btservice@betamedia.com.tw

總 經 銷 / 時報文化出版企業股份有限公司
地　　址 / 桃園縣龜山鄉萬壽路二段 351 號
電　　話 / (02) 2306-6842

出版日期 / 2007年4月初版一刷
定　　價 / 350元
ISBN：978-957-729-642-9

Biz English for Busy People—Job Hunting
Copyright 2007 by Quentin Brand
Published by Beta Multimedia Publishing

喚醒你的英文語感 ！

對折後釘好，直接寄回即可！

| 廣　告　回　信 |
| 北區郵政管理局登記證 |
| 北 台 字 第 1 4 2 5 6 號 |
| 免　貼　郵　票 |

100 台北市中正區館前路12號11樓

 貝塔語言出版 收
Beta Multimedia Publishing

寄件者住址 □□□

謝謝您購買本書！！

貝塔語言擁有最優良之英文學習書籍，為提供您最佳的英語學習資訊，您可填妥此表後寄回（免貼郵票）將可不定期收到本公司最新發行書訊及活動訊息！

姓名：＿＿＿＿＿＿＿＿＿＿＿ 性別：□男 □女 生日：＿＿＿年＿＿＿月＿＿＿日

電話：(公)＿＿＿＿＿＿＿＿＿＿(宅)＿＿＿＿＿＿＿＿＿＿(手機)＿＿＿＿＿＿＿＿＿

電子信箱：＿＿＿＿＿＿＿＿＿＿＿＿＿＿＿＿＿＿＿＿＿＿＿

學歷：□高中職含以下 □專科 □大學 □研究所含以上

職業：□金融 □服務 □傳播 □製造 □資訊 □軍公教 □出版
　　　□自由 □教育 □學生 □其他

職級：□企業負責人 □高階主管 □中階主管 □職員 □專業人士

1. 您購買的書籍是？＿＿＿＿＿＿＿＿＿＿＿＿＿＿＿＿＿

2. 您從何處得知本產品？(可複選)

　　　□書店 □網路 □書展 □校園活動 □廣告信函 □他人推薦 □新聞報導 □其他

3. 您覺得本產品價格：

　　　□偏高 □合理 □偏低

4. 請問目前您每週花了多少時間學英語？

　　　□ 不到十分鐘 □ 十分鐘以上，但不到半小時 □ 半小時以上，但不到一小時

　　　□ 一小時以上，但不到兩小時 □ 兩個小時以上 □ 不一定

5. 通常在選擇語言學習書時，哪些因素是您會考慮的？

　　　□ 封面 □ 內容、實用性 □ 品牌 □ 媒體、朋友推薦 □ 價格 □ 其他＿＿＿＿＿

6. 市面上您最需要的語言書種類為？

　　　□ 聽力 □ 閱讀 □ 文法 □ 口說 □ 寫作 □ 其他＿＿＿＿＿＿

7. 通常您會透過何種方式選購語言學習書籍？

　　　□ 書店門市 □ 網路書店 □ 郵購 □ 直接找出版社 □ 學校或公司團購

　　　□ 其他＿＿＿＿＿＿＿

8. 給我們的建議：＿＿＿＿＿＿＿＿＿＿＿＿＿＿＿＿＿＿＿＿

＿＿＿＿＿＿＿＿＿＿＿＿＿＿＿＿＿＿＿＿＿＿＿＿＿＿＿＿

喚醒你的英文語感！

Get a Feel for English !